*A Joke Goes A Long Way
In The Country*

A Joke Goes A Long Way
In The Country

by

Alannah Hopkin

Hamish Hamilton
London

The extract from Sean Jennett's *Cork and Kerry* on
p.19 is reproduced by kind permission of the Estate
of the late Sean Jennett and B.T. Batsford Ltd.

The lines from 'This is the Only Poem' (as published
in *The Energy of Slaves*, Jonathan Cape) on p.26
are reproduced by kind permission of Leonard
Cohen.

First published in Great Britain 1982
by Hamish Hamilton Ltd
Garden House 57–59 Long Acre London WC2E 9JZ

British Library Cataloguing in Publication Data
Hopkin, Alannah
   A joke goes a long way in the country.
   I. Title
   823'.914[F]   PR6059.0/

ISBN 0-241-10798-9

Photoset by Rowland Phototypesetting Limited
Printed in Great Britain by
St Edmundsbury Press
Bury St Edmunds, Suffolk

To my parents with thanks for everything

First, never go against the best light you have; secondly, take care that your light be not darkness.
Bishop Wilson (1663–1755)
Maxims

There is a space within which we can make something of that which has been made of us.
Jean Paul Sartre (1905–1980)

PROLOGUE

I shall go back to London and rest awhile, for I am
very tired. Then some day I shall take a train from Paddington.
At Fishguard I shall go aboard the little liner that takes
you to Cork. I have never been there, but I am told that,
having travelled all night, you wake in a wide harbour with
a loveliness to make you wonder.

Howard Spring
My Son, My Son

Just once in a longish while you can write yourself an
order for a pair of seven league boots, and you travel
inhumanly far in next to no time. It is only 8 hours or
thereabouts from Fishguard to Cork, but on the quay there
in Cork I knew at once what kind of boots I had on. For
whatever a person feels about Ireland – likes it, loathes it,
or it merely blurs on him – it's a long way from England in
all directions. Here and there it is a little nearer to
America, but it's a long way from there too.

Claud Cockburn
Cockburn Sums Up

It was raining again. Morning's mist had lifted only to be replaced at midday by a thin drizzle. The drizzle had spent the afternoon getting heavier and by five o'clock a steady grey downpour was lashing the granite slates on the roofs of Castletownbere. Up in Bethlehem even the sheep were taking shelter, and everybody stayed indoors.

Alex had been sitting all afternoon with her feet up on the sofa staring into the turf fire and stroking the cat who dozed on her knee. She was listening intently to the different sounds made by the rain as it dripped in random rhythms against the regular ticking and chiming of the mantel clock.

Every so often she would disturb the cat by getting up to check the effect of a broken gutter above the back window and look through the twisting channels of rain at the fresh greenness of the various ferns and mosses growing out of the shiny black rock behind the house.

She had rearranged the furniture in the first-floor sitting room so that while her feet toasted near the fire she could see the masts of the trawlers from her sofa, and, on those rare occasions when it was not raining too hard, the top of Bear Island beyond the masts.

They said it was the coldest, wettest July in living memory and that suited her well. She spent most of her days lying on the sofa not thinking. The floor around her was littered with discarded books, Seamus Heaney, J. G. Farrell, Aidan Higgins, Bernard Maclaverty, Desmond Hogan, Julia O'Faolain, Jennifer Johnston, most of them resting face down, open at the page where she'd lost interest. She preferred to look at the burning turf and listen to the rain.

When it was not raining she often stood at the front window looking across the grey choppy sea to Bear Island and the hazy silhouettes of purple mountains on the other side of Bantry Bay. It made her feel uneasy, as if there were something she'd forgotten to do, somewhere else she should be. She had still not settled. She never looked out of the window for long, but preferred to go downstairs and throw on her yellow oilskin jacket and walk briskly around the quay, past the incongruous new Fir and Mná, noting trawlers just in from Vigo and Finisterre and Coruña tied up beside the familiar Castletown-bere boats.

Sometimes she prowled around the house from room to room disturbing the light film of dust on the old pieces of furniture and pulling sticky cobwebs off the windows with her fingers. The piano was out of tune, the radiogram and the tall mahogany standard lamp didn't work. The armchairs were lumpy and dressed with shabby anti-macassars which looked worse than the threadbare patches they were supposed to cover. The staircase smelt even more musty than the rest, and on the first-floor landing plaster was flaking off the wall and lay in white heaps on the black-painted wooden boards.

She always used to sleep in the front attic bedroom which had a high bedstead so that, if she left the blind open, when she woke up she could see the sea and the mountains across the bay through the dormer window. But there were loose slates on the roof above it and birds were nesting in the gutter and some nights the sighs and creakings kept her awake and made her imagination race, sending her into a cold sweat. It dawned around four, so only if she went to bed late after several whiskeys did she use that front attic bedroom. Other nights she used a tiny low-beamed back bedroom which had only a lead skylight set into the sloping roof and a view on to the rocky untended back garden where hedges of fuchsia and bright pink tea roses grew wild.

She seldom got up before midday, and waited till about six in the evening before eating. So today, soon after the clock chimed for half past five, she went down to the kitchen.

She buttered two slices of soda bread, cut a tomato into quarters, made a pot of tea while the egg boiled and sat down at the oil-cloth-covered table. As she was eating she faced up to the major decision of the day: which bar to visit tonight.

She narrowed it down from the dozen or so within easy walking distance to either Shanahan's for a game of darts, or the Berehaven Inn for a chat with Tomás and maybe a song from old Pat.

As she poured her second cup of tea she decided it would be Shanahan's.

*   *   *

'I just don't fucking believe it. I saw it with my own eyes and I still don't fucking believe it.'

'Hugh!' She was running to keep up with him, stumbling along the suburban pavement in the darkness and the rain. 'Hugh, listen to me for godsake. . . .'

'Like a common whore. Worse than a common whore. My Alex. Screwing on the coats in the bedroom. Screwing a fucking Trot. Jesus Christ, I don't believe it. I thought you had more class.'

'Hugh, I'm sorry. I didn't think. He's an old friend, it just happened, I must have been drunk. Hugh, please listen to me. Hugh, oh, Hugh!' She started to cry, noisily. 'I didn't mean to hurt you.'

'Hurt me! You've just killed the best relationship you'll ever have. I thought we fucking meant something. I thought this was supposed to be different. Jesus Christ, you stink.'

'Hugh, I didn't mean to hurt you.'

He stopped walking. As she caught up with him he swung his arm out slowly and slapped her hard on the face.

'Don't you ever say that to me again. Ever.'

She stumbled backwards, trembling from the shock. 'Hugh' – in a low pleading voice.

'Get away from me.' He changed from anger to scorn: 'You spoilt mixed-up bitch. Go back to Digger and the goddamn party and leave me alone. And I hope your cunt fucking rots.'

*   *   *

Alex is not a common whore, even if Hugh was to some extent justified in accusing her of behaving like one. She is indeed the same Alex who, less than a year later, found herself leading such a quiet exemplary life in a small town in West Cork.

When Digger had her on the coats she was a bit drunk, although of course that's no excuse. And she could never have predicted that Hugh would decide to leave early and go looking for his coat in the very bedroom where she and Digger were celebrating their unexpected meeting that evening, the first meeting after ending an affair some eight years before, during their first year at university.

Alex had only known Hugh for about six months, and one reason why things had gone so far with Digger was that Hugh always ignored her at parties and concentrated on getting drunk. She was fed up with that, and now realised that she had subconsciously been looking for a way to break away from Hugh for quite some time. But Hugh could also be very charming, and when he wasn't too drunk Alex enjoyed his company. She was also flattered by his devotion. An unmarried forty-two-year-old features editor was a rare find, even if he did work for a lurid tabloid. She enjoyed lazy weekends at his comfortable flat, dinner parties with his more civilised friends, pub crawls with the less civilised ones, trips to the country in his car and so on. It was pleasant enough to drift along without worrying about where it was all leading, and if she hadn't been caught in the act with Digger it might have gone on for many months.

Hugh was far closer to the mark when he called Alex a 'spoilt mixed-up bitch' than when he accused her of behaving like a common whore. She thought she was fairly high-principled, especially when she compared herself with a lot of her friends. But high principles led more often to confusion than to clarity. She'd been brought up a Catholic, and in spite of some radical disagreements with the Church (mostly about sex) still considered herself one. This combined uneasily with the residue of what she called her Epicurean phase, which had dictated spontaneous indulgence in the pleasures of the flesh.

She liked to think that her education at a progressive convent had left her with an admirable habit of moral introspection, and the ability to be honest with herself, however painful the process. But what in fact happened was that she quite happily followed her own instincts, only reflecting afterwards on the consequences of her action. It was then that she adapted her beliefs to fit whatever circumstance she found herself in, and so she neatly avoided the need for absolutes.

So, when Hugh left her stranded on a pavement in Hampstead in the early hours of a very rainy morning, her conscience immediately went into overdrive. Within minutes her tears had dried as she justified her actions. Hugh was well aware that she refused to promise fidelity to anyone. She had tried it once for three years while she was living with a man called Henry. Her horrified reaction on discovering that Henry, while mouthing the same promises, had been screwing everyone in reach, had convinced her that fidelity was detrimental to good relationships. Her discovery of Henry's unfaithfulness had driven a wedge between them, destroying what had otherwise been a reasonably pleasant set-up.

Nevertheless, she still felt guilty about screwing Digger while being Hugh's guest at the party, and put this down to (a) bad manners and (b) having unnecessarily hurt Hugh. However, that was done, Hugh was finished as a lover, and she was on her own again.

It was just over two years since Alex had left the man called Henry, and she still enjoyed being unattached. She was constantly surprised at her ability to attract interesting new lovers, though by the age of twenty-six she should have learnt to accept that men found her physically attractive. She was a slight, small-boned person, with a pale pointed face which was constantly changing, betraying her slightest shift in mood. She gave the impression of being intense to the point of hyperactive, only because every action of her scrupulous mind showed on her face and in her gestures. She was a slow, laborious thinker, and the obvious usually took a long time to dawn on her. But, meanwhile, all the thought processes were in evidence, so she always looked on the point of saying something interesting, though she seldom did. She was just thinking. With the added advantage of well-cut black hair and strange green eyes it was not surprising that men liked her.

Having coped with the demands of her conscience, Alex then turned to immediate practical problems, and moved under a lamp-post which shed some light on the contents of her handbag. She was not going back to the party. Digger had her number and would call. That was enough. Her purse turned out to contain not enough money for a taxi, so there was a long walk ahead. Luckily she liked walking, and she was also fond of rain.

As she set out on her trek through the dark wet streets she consoled herself with the thought that she was far better off alone than in the company of a man who was so inherently vulgar as to be able to come out with the phrase 'I hope your cunt fucking rots' and sound as if he meant it.

EXPOSITION

Sorrow and sadness bitterness grief
Memories I have of you
Won't leave me in peace
My mind is running back
To the west coast of Clear
Thinking of you
And the times we had there

Castletownbear was empty of people when we drove in
and parked in the square. It lay under the somnolence
typical of Irish small towns on a weekday that is not a
market day and when the men are out on the land. The shops
around the square looked old-fashioned and dusty and as
though they seldom had customers. The two and three storied
houses with slate roofs and plastered fronts showed small
variation, though some were distinguished by stone frames
around the windows. But on the quay fronting the square
there was a lot of construction machinery for the building
of new quays or wharves, and there was that indisputable
symbol of progress in Ireland, a new ladies' and gents'.
Industry, including a freezing plant to serve the trawlers
coming into Bearhaven, had come to the town. In the harbour
a long and graceful brand-new bridge spanned the channel
between the mainland and Dinish Island, where a new fishmeal
factory has been built.

Bear Haven, between Bear Island and the mainland, was
a centre of the British fleet up to the year 1938, when,
as the result of an agreement with the Irish government,
the British left. This agreement was opposed by certain
British politicians, notably Churchill, and when the Second
World War broke out in 1939 these people felt that their
attitude had been justified. Churchill, who was sometimes
strangely stupid, wanted to recover the use of Bear Haven
(and of Loch Swilly) by force, so that Britain migh have a
base convenient for action against U-boats in the Atlantic.
The result of such an action would have been to tie up
large numbers of British troops in Ireland, to dry up the
sources of Irish recruits for the British Army (there were
many thousands of these) and to give the RAF and the Navy
immense new tasks in the defence of Ireland against the
Germans. It came to nothing in the end, but if it had
come about it might have been the factor that tipped the
balance against England.

Bear Island, accessible by boat, still has the remains
of the British establishment, and an earlier defence, a

Martello tower, built when the enemy of the British was not a corporal with a funny moustache, but a different and earlier corporal with a funny hat.

Cork and Kerry by Sean
Jennett, London 1977

Alex shared a flat in Chelsea with a girl called Jane. She and Jane had been at school together, but Jane had never been a close friend and still wasn't. She was two years older than Alex, and had always been one of the 'big girls' to her. When they ran into each other again Jane was in mid-divorce, and looking for a congenial undemanding person to live in her spare bedroom and pay rent. Alex was desperately searching for a room, having just decided to leave Henry, and sharing with someone like Jane, whom she knew slightly, was far more attractive than plunging into the world of flat-share small ads.

She was still a bit overwhelmed by Jane, and the two-year age difference, which would have been unimportant with anyone else, became exaggerated because of memories of school. Added to that, the fact that Jane had managed to get married and divorced and buy her own flat by the age of twenty-six made her seem intimidatingly well-organised to Alex.

Jane was a good-looking glossy blonde, but Alex thought her classic way of dressing made her look far too old. She had a very affected manner which was meant to give an impression of great sophistication, which Alex put up with because she assumed that Jane was hellishly insecure underneath it all. Even so, Jane's bossiness and posing managed to keep Alex in awe of her for a long time.

The split with Henry and the move to Jane's happened at exactly the moment when Alex, after some months of unemployment and typing jobs, started to earn a living (if a meagre one) as a freelance journalist.

Her transition from Academe to Grub Street via the dole queue was by no means a unique and sensational achievement. Henry was a press photographer, so through him she knew some helpful people. The lack of opportunities for arts graduates in the usual refuges of publishing and teaching meant that a number of people found it easier to give up searching for a 'proper job', and instead start work in a precarious but enjoyable way by researching and writing for magazines and newspapers and books. Alex had lived for so long on student grants that the lack of a regular pay packet did not bother her, and she was quite disproportionately pleased with the small amounts that she earned. She enjoyed the constant sensation of living off miracles where others would only have felt horror at wondering where the next cheque was coming from.

She was not serious about her career. She saw journalism as a fairly pleasant way of earning money to pay the bills, and sometimes considered doing a bit of part-time teaching in adult education to keep up her reading, but never quite got around to it. She'd always assumed that she'd be a writer of some kind, because it was the only thing she seemed to be good at, and she believed that journalism was useful training for that vague future ambition.

She was not interested in getting married, or having children or buying a flat or a car or sailing round the world or writing the definitive biography of J. G. Farrell, although she occasionally considered all those possibilities and hoped she'd get around to them one of these days. She often thought about going to live in Ireland, but with a similar lack of urgency or attention to details. She had spent all her childhood holidays at her grandmother's house in Kinsale near Cork city, and later in Castletownbere in the far west of Cork near the border with Kerry, where her widowed aunt Kate lived.

She had very nearly settled in Cork instead of going to live with Jane. It was a close thing. She went to stay with Kate immediately after leaving Henry, and it was then that she'd met a man called Tomás. Tomás had heard that she liked sailing, and as they joked one evening over a few jars in Shanahan's, a local bar cum general store, he decided that he liked Alex. She was mildly bored with staying at Kate's and subject to fits of depression about Henry, so when Tom suddenly asked her if she'd help him to deliver a yacht up to Kinsale the next morning she was happy to agree. She expected no more than a nice sail in good company.

On the way up the coast they tied up in the north harbour of Cape Clear Island for the first night, fell passionately in love, and declared themselves weatherbound for the next ten days. The idyll ended when Alex insisted on going back to London instead of staying on in Castletownbere and being dependent on Tom while she found what would probably be a menial job. She had only just discovered that in London she could make a living in journalism, and to leave for Castletownbere at that moment would have felt like running away from a challenge. More importantly (it seemed at the time) she could not face committing herself to another long-term relationship, let alone marriage, as Tom was suggesting, so soon after Henry.

Tom did not understand and turned up melodramatically distraught on Jane's doorstep one night soon after her return. A week later they both accepted that Tomás could not settle in London, and Alex could not move to Ireland, and a not very amicable stalemate was declared. They met on Alex's visits to Kate, but both felt misunderstood by the other. The grand passion degenerated into angry concern on each side for how the other was wasting a life.

Alex and Jane sometimes had chats about what Jane referred to as their 'love life' and their 'social life'. Each had their own set of friends and they seldom mixed. Jane worked in a Mayfair art gallery and Alex considered her friends intolerably stuffy. But Jane, who blatantly chose to reserve her affections for rich older men who would spoil her and adore her, could be amusingly cynical about her adventures. Alex felt naive and gauche by contrast, yet Jane seemed to be fascinated, often even impressed by Alex's friends.

Jane enjoyed the story of Digger and Hugh. It was most unusual for their worlds to produce coincidences, but their discussion confirmed that Alex's Digger was the same Digger that Jane had met a few weeks before at a political dinner party. As for Hugh, Jane now revealed that she had always mistrusted his Scottish working class background, and suspected him of having a chip on his shoulder. His resort to violence, she said, betrayed his origins.

It was the sort of comment Alex had got used to living with, much as she disliked it. Jane's reactionary political attitudes were another reason why their chats never went much beyond social and love life. Alex believed the compromise was justified because she was, in a manner of speaking, a guest in Jane's house. And she assured herself it was all part of Jane's pose anyway, because Jane was essentially a very nice person, considerate and kind, and no one that nice could be a true reactionary. It was the same sort of enjoyment in shocking – a form of *épater les bourgeois* – that made Jane so amusing when she talked about her amorous pursuits.

Another reason that Jane was glad to see the end of Hugh was that it meant that Alex could now see more of Andy, one of the men that she'd been two-timing Hugh with. Andy was from Kinsale, and he and Alex were childhood friends. He was now starting to make a name for himself in London as a pop singer. Jane had been astounded to come back one night and find the famous Andy O'Sullivan lying on her sitting room floor with Alex, listening to Beethoven's Eroica at full volume.

It was the first time Alex had produced anyone rich or famous. Jane was starting to feel sorry for Alex in an almost motherly way. She had never seemed quite to recover from the Tomás fiasco and apparently never fell in love with anyone, nor had any glittering invitations. Jane believed that Andy was the sort of person to take Alex into the right circles, and introduce her to the right sort of people. Now that Hugh was out of the way Alex had no excuse for not getting as much as possible out of Andy.

On a rainy morning in November about three weeks after the fight with Hugh, Alex was lying in bed staring at the alarm clock on her bedside table and trying to work up enough interest in the day ahead to make herself get up. She was doing this by means of approximate mental calculations of how much money she could earn before six o'clock. She had a fairly lucrative commission to update part of a shopping guide which a friend of hers was editing, and she would be paid according to the number of places she visited or spoke to on the phone. She was calculating away on the basis of a six o'clock deadline, when she remembered that today was Tuesday not Wednesday, so she had two days left not one, so if she moved like mad today and tomorrow morning, and typed like mad tomorrow afternoon, she could make a significant amount of money, worth braving the freezing cold early morning for. . . .

As she jumped out of bed she heard the bathroom door slam shut, and stood poised for a moment, cursing under her breath. Jane began to run a bath, Alex looked longingly at her bed once more, and then decided to get dressed straight away. She looked around the room for her clothes, which she usually folded neatly on a ladder-back chair. For some reason she had put them away last night, and as she opened the closet she remembered throwing them into her laundry bag to remind her that today was laundrette day.

She looked at the sparse hangers and decided against jeans. She had to go and see people, black cords would be better, she raided the laundry bag for a black shirt and pulled her black sweater down from the closet shelf.

'Boots,' she muttered, pulling back the curtain an inch or so to confirm that the rain looked as if it was settling in for the day. She only had dark brown boots, from the year before last, and a very tatty raincoat which she'd bought in a sale during her final year at university.

'Bloody hell,' she muttered. 'I must buy some damn clothes, this is ridiculous. And a woolly dressing-gown.' Every time they had a cold snap Jane talked piously about getting an estimate for central heating, but somehow the weather always changed before she came to any firm decision.

Alex sighed as she dressed, remembering that she had nothing to do that evening. Maybe, she thought, someone nice that I haven't seen for ages will phone up and ask me out to dinner. Or maybe I'll stay in and write a bit in my journal. Oh, hell. . . . That was often her intention, but she seldom managed it.

She was feeling listless and very cold. The kettle took ages to boil, perhaps they were running out of gas again. They cooked on a two-burner camping stove because Jane was still wrangling with her ex-husband about a cooker. It had turned into a desperately important matter of principle that he should supply her with one. It was the only reason she ever communicated with him. Meanwhile she and Alex spent a ridiculous amount of money on cans of gas and alternative gadgets like the toaster and the pressure cooker. About time we got an electric kettle, thought Alex, and a coffee percolator. Christmas was coming up soon, she'd better start hinting to her parents.

She was further irritated by the sight of Jane's boiled egg sitting in her little egg-boiling saucepan, and two slices of wholemeal bread on a plate. It all looked so smug and sensible and well-organised, everything that Alex was not in the early morning. And what about getting some real coffee, she thought as she spooned instant stuff into a mug. I don't know why I bother to bloody work if I don't bother to spend the money on things I like. Holy shit. She seldom swore aloud, but often thought in strings of childish obscenities.

The bathroom door opened and Jane ran squealing down the corridor to her room wrapped in a scanty pink towel. 'The water's just boiled,' shouted Alex, to prove that she was out of bed. 'Shall I turn your egg on?'

'Please, darling. Oooh, I'm frozen, this is dreadful. I must phone those central heating chaps as soon as I get to work.' Fortunately she could not see the 'Like hell you will' expression on Alex's face. She left the egg on high and took her coffee back to the desk in the corner of her room, to organise her day's work.

The cardboard file containing the shopping guide notes was under a sheaf of lined loose-leaf paper covered in her sprawling longhand. Her journal. She remembered now, she'd been writing in it the night before, a bottle of wine by her side, examining a kind of angry exhilaration that had come over her because of a poem she'd been reading. She'd copied out the closing lines of the poem, and read them through again as she tidied up:

> I didn't kill myself
> when things went wrong
> I didn't turn
> to drugs or teaching
> I tried to sleep
> but when I couldn't sleep
> I learned to write
> I learned to write
> what might be read
> on nights like this
> by one like me

Not bad, she thought, looking at it again in the clear light of day (i.e. minus the slight alcoholic haze in which she'd copied it out). It was close, but she'd never considered killing herself, and had no inclination to turn to drugs, unless you counted wine. Or Shanahan's after hours, she added to herself. She smiled grimly, some of her bad humour lifting.

As she sat at her desk and faced the prospect of an eight-hour stint interrogating antique shop owners to assess their suitability for inclusion in a guide book of London for the rich, she allowed herself a fraction of a second in which to question whether Shanahan's and Castletownbere and the Beara peninsula and even West Cork in general actually existed. She decided they must, because in precisely twenty minutes the 9.50 flight to Cork would leave from Heathrow arriving one drink (two if you're pushy) and fifty-five tedious minutes later to unload its passengers in the middle of a fresh green field covered with springy grass in surprisingly balmy air and leaving them to walk into the terminal building and collect their luggage from the one trundling conveyor belt and pass the time of day with the customs officers before walking through the swing doors to face the scrutiny of a crowd of ruddy, searching faces and there is one that breaks from anxiety into a smile and moves forward with open arms saying, 'Alex Buckley, plague of my life. . . .'

She shook her head violently to get rid of the vivid images and muttered, 'Oh, shit, you're not usually like this, gerragrip willya. . . .'

'Byeeeee.' Jane opened the door of Alex's room and saw her huddled over the phone about to lift the receiver and smiled at her in just the way, thought Alex, that anyone who's just had a bath, eaten a boiled egg with wholemeal toast and bullshitted about getting central heating installed, would smile.

'Will you be in this evening, darling? At about cocktail time?'

(I don't believe it! 'Cocktail time.' Holy shit!)

Alex stifled her horror and replied pleasantly enough, 'Oh, I suppose so, I'll be back by about 5.30 and I'm not really planning to go out until. . . .'

'Super. In that case, if Justin phones tell him I'm not back and you don't know where to get me, but if it's David tell him I'm staying late at the gallery to have a few drinks with some of Pippa's friends and if he'd care to join us he's absolutely welcome, but in any case I'll be home about eight unless I go out to dinner with David, so tell Justin you've simply no idea but why doesn't he try again at eight. Of course if I do go out to dinner with David you'll get landed with Justin twice, but I hope. . . .'

'That's okay, I love lying to Justin.'

28

'Oh . . . well, thanks awfully anyway, see you later, bye eee.'

Oh, hell, thought Alex! She probably thought I was being sarcastic.

*   *   *

Extract from Alex's journal dated late November:

I remember the day had the most unlikely start. I got cross about Jane's boiled egg and then I had a bad attack of Castletownbere nostalgia. But by five o'clock I was in a much better mood, really quite pleased with myself. I'd got a lot of work done, and the final write-ups would put me well into the black for the next couple of weeks.

So I felt entitled to a bottle of cold white wine when I got back that evening after checking antique shops. I like to lie on the sofa and sip wine and listen to very loud music once I've finished working. It's one of the few nice habits I picked up while I was living with Henry. But, in any case, I manage to justify bottles of wine on most of the evenings I stay in alone, because the change of mood it brings is some guarantee against boredom.

Usually I relax to reggae music, but that night the reggae didn't work. It wasn't just because I had to get up twice to deal with Justin and then David on the phone. The music suddenly meant nothing to me any more. The hypnotic beat and the barely comprehensible voice-overs that I used to love died on me. Even though I was alone I felt embarrassed by how banal it was. And this after years of preaching at my friends, even Jane, about the wonders of reggae. It was music of sorts, and I like most music, but it now had only a remote ethnic interest, it didn't get through to me at all.

Then a strange thing happened. I went over to the records, which were neatly divided into two stacks leaning against the wall. There was Jane's small stack of recently-bought middle of the road stuff, and my own bigger collection assembled over the last twelve years, that I'm quite proud of. No music lover has yet looked through it without both groaning at the awfulness of some of it (I'm quite fond of American country music and sentimental Irish ballads) and exclaiming at the recherché excesses of other parts of it – like six different recordings of Albinoni's Adagio, and lots of other baroque music as well as all that blasted reggae.

I try to keep the stack in some kind of order so that I can find what I want without getting distracted by things that I like but haven't heard for ages. But inevitably certain records work their way to the back and stay there. It was at the back that I started looking that night, with a quite uncanny feeling that I was going to put my hand on exactly the right record to take over from the reggae. What I pulled out was an LP called 'Planxty' which had been given to me by an American I'd met the previous summer. She'd thought that as I was Irish I'd like it. I played it once, sneered at what I thought was its pseudo-Celtishness (not in front of the American of course who was nice) and put it at the back of the stack.

But that night, halfway through a litre of white wine, I fished it out without even thinking about what I was looking for, listened to it again and sank back into the music. It was perfectly right. There was one contemporary song that I especially liked – 'The West Coast of Clare'. It was odd, because I've never been to Clare.

With the surprise of discovering 'Planxty' to be so good I overdid the relaxation, and suddenly it was eight o'clock, the wine bottle was empty and the phone was ringing. I assumed it would be Justin, and dithered about whether to answer it or not. There was a very long outside chance that it might be Digger or Andy or someone else for me, so I picked it up. It was Justin. By then I couldn't remember what Jane had told me to say, so I said she was still out. Sneaky bugger invited me to dinner instead, which is entirely against the code of practice (house rules about men that Jane and I agreed on before I moved in). I was a bit tempted, but I'm very glad I didn't go when I think of all I would have missed.

I went to the pub instead because I was feeling chatty. Our local is quite unusual for London. The regular crowd are mostly older than me, but we all know one another and sometimes go to parties in one another's houses. There are some really heavy boozers there, but things never get out of hand. As they're mostly older than me they are also a lot richer than me, so I let them buy me drinks and seldom reciprocate. So, although no one plays darts and there's no music, it's a good place to visit on the odd nights when I decide to pursue the narcotic pleasures of alcohol beyond a few glasses of wine at home.

It was an ordinary sort of evening. I talked to Kay about her dog, and drifted over to join Bill and Doug and eavesdrop on their discussion of whether Jill was having it off with Kay's husband or not, and they bought me a drink. Then I was surrounded by a younger crowd from an advertising agency who were celebrating someone's birthday in their newly-discovered 'real Chelsea pub', and they bought me several drinks, as a token gesture towards mixing with the locals, I remember thinking.

I slipped off home on my own just before closing time. I'm quite good at that. Jane still wasn't in so I went and put on 'Planxty' again rather loud, and collapsed back on the Chesterfield, reflecting that, apart from having relaxed myself, it had been a rather pointless evening, disconcerting in the sudden rejection of reggae and discovery of 'Planxty', but pointless in the visit to the pub. But there wasn't really much else I could have done. Eaten a decent meal and watched TV on whichever channel worked best, or eaten and read, or eaten and washed my hair, or made phone calls to Digger and Andy and other friends who'd either be depressed, out, or watching TV. All seemed just as pointless as going to the pub.

In spite of 'Planxty' I was starting to get a bit down, when, lo and behold, the telephone rang. Just after closing time, so I assumed it would be Hugh, who had got into the habit of phoning me at about that time of night and reminding me of what a wonderful relationship I had thrown away and what a stupid bitch I was. He never upset me, but I was a bit worried about the habitually sodden state he had got himself into.

At first I hesitated at the phone bell, wondering if I should pretend to be out, then I decided that I was in the best possible mood for dealing with Hugh's maudlin self-pity and would enjoy a bit of a confrontation after so much polite mindless chat in the local. I picked it up and got phone box pips and was shouting bored sarcastic 'halloes' when a voice came through, a Castletownbere voice, saying softly, anxiously, 'Hallo, Buckley, hallo?'

I couldn't believe it. I knew it was Tomás O'Suilleabháin and I couldn't believe it. He was saying he was at Paddington Station, and something about just having sailed someone's yacht over (and I thought how crazy, in November, how typically Tomás) and could he stay the night, wanted to see me, was I alone, was it too late, Falmouth train delayed, difficult crossing, dead tired.

I told him to come straight over and went rushing around in circles, into the kitchen to make some coffee then back to the bedroom to put on some make-up and into the sitting room to clear up the ashtrays, and all the time forgetting to finish what I'd started.

Hearing from him out of the blue like that struck me as extra strange because after months of managing not to think about Tom at all it had been his face that I'd seen so vividly in my mind that very morning, meeting me at Cork airport. I only hear odd bits of news about him from my aunt Kate who lives in the main square of Castletownbere and often chats with him. I couldn't even remember whether we were on speaking terms or not, but he obviously thought we were, so that was good enough for me.

When the bell rang unexpectedly soon, I ran to open the door, pulled it back with a big smile, and immediately thought I must be going mad, or if not I damn soon would.

It was Hugh who staggered in, carrying a transparent plastic bag from Frankfurt airport in which I could see a bottle of whiskey, a carton of cigarettes and a bottle of Ma Griffe. He was almost incoherent.

'Eh, you're glad to see me then.' I'd been so dumbfounded I'd forgotten to stop smiling. He placed the perfume in my hands and crushed me to him with one arm. He stank of whiskey.

'I've come for a quick one. You'll like it, you always liked it. . . .' He went straight to my bedroom muttering to himself. Then he shouted affectionately, 'Come here, you silly old tart.'

I couldn't move, couldn't think, I just stood there in the entrance hall.

'We're going to fuck now, two days in Frankfurt, met a whore there, reminded me of you, bus coming in from

Heathrow, black night pissing bloody rain – I'm half-pissed in case you hadn't noticed – (laughter) all on my own, no one to go home to, thought I'd go and see my Alex, missed you, I've bloody missed you, Alex, you had no right . . . half-cut tough shit Hugh Fitzsimon, lonely and I missed you.'

He ranted on and on, laughing at himself one minute, and being miserable the next, and I was scared. He'd often threatened on the phone to come to the flat and 'get a leg over' as he chose to put it, but I always managed to talk him out of it, and never thought that he would.

I was still standing at the door when he reappeared wearing only his purple underpants, and lunged at me. I dodged him, he went sprawling on the floor and cursed me horribly, so I did the only thing I could think of – ran out into the street and slammed the front door behind me. I was sure Hugh would need another drink and maybe even stop to put on some clothes before he opened the front door, so I ran up the square and hid on the front steps of the corner house where I had shelter from the rain and could watch my own front door, hopefully without Hugh seeing me.

It gave me a moment to think. Jane was with David and it was impossible to know whether they'd sleep at his place or hers, so I couldn't rely on them coming back to rescue me. And it wasn't something I'd like to land them with either. So I was hoping Tomás would turn up first. The only thing to do would be to tell him the truth – that I was locked out and my bedroom was occupied by a drunken half-crazy ex-boyfriend who might get violent. He wasn't going to like it. I was relying heavily on the belief that besides being lovers we were also very good friends. Surely he wouldn't go off and leave me to sort it out alone. I shivered and felt sick. Tom can be very unpredictable, that had once been part of his charm. It was not impossible that he'd change his mind and book into a hotel and come over in the morning instead. He's like that about arrangements.

I saw my front door open. Hugh came out wearing my pink silk dressing-gown. I ducked. He shouted my name a few times, then I heard the door slam again.

I shivered for a few more minutes, and all sorts of plans to get help were half-formed and rejected, Kay and Daniel from the pub, the people in the basement flat, even the police. I felt humiliated by not being able to handle it myself, and I had just decided that if Tom didn't turn up soon I'd go back in and face up to being groped and maybe screwed by Hugh rather than ask for help from anyone else, when Tom's taxi drew up outside the flat.

He had his yellow oilskin jacket on, and sea boots, and he was carrying an old duffel bag and as he stood at the window paying the driver his hair hung over his forehead in wet black curls and dripped on to his beard. He looked so familiar that I didn't even register how strange it was to see him in London again. That's always been part of what makes Tom so attractive. Ever since I first saw him in Shanahan's he's had a totally familiar face. It's not that he looks like anyone else, he just looks as if he's someone I've always known, since I was a kid or something.

Anyway, to my absolute horror as soon as I reached Tom, instead of explaining it all to him, I burst into tears and could hardly talk at all. He led me up the steps to the front door, treating me like a child as he so often does, and I told him as best I could about Hugh and being locked out. I was terrified that Hugh would open the door before Tom understood what was going on. At first I thought he was angry:

'Jesus, woman, you're a hard case altogether. When will you ever get sense?'

Then he smiled at me and kissed me on my forehead in the very offhand way that he always used to, for no special reason except that he was in a good mood.

'Tom, I'm sorry about this. I feel so stupid.'

'You are, plague of my life. Not only are you stupid, you're a total looney and you'll never get sense. I don't know what I'm going to do with you at all.'

This was like a chorus between me and Tom, one of us was always saying it to the other, but this time I just laughed and said, 'Let's get it over with.'

Hugh took a while to open the door once I'd knocked, and I began to worry that he might have passed out, but when I looked through the letter box I could see him coming down the hall, a drink in one hand, a cigarette in the other, still wearing my pink dressing-gown. He was looking at the floor, and at first he didn't notice Tomás at all. He only became aware of him when I'd shut the front door and the three of us were standing in the hall. Tomás was taking off his jacket and shaking the rain from it on to the door-mat.

'Who's that?' Hugh asked me, looking as if he owned the place. 'You picked him up in the street?' He advanced on me, one hand raised in a threat, and I backed away, hiding behind Tomás.

'Hugh, I want you to leave please. This is Tomás, a very old friend of mine from Castletownbere that I told you about once.'

'Ah ha! The fucking paddy! The off-shore bog trotter! What the fuck does he think he's doing here then, eh?'

'She's asked would you leave.'

'Begosh and begorrah, would I leave. . . .'

Hugh got thumped for that, Tom's very sensitive about people in London laughing at his accent. The drink and the cigarette went flying but Hugh managed to stay on his feet and within seconds he and Tom were wrestling their way up the hall. I heard my dressing-gown split, and then Hugh crashed against the hall table, knocking off a vase of dried flowers and Jane's bills. He started to get up and Tom went for him again and I began screaming at both of them to stop before they hurt each other and wrecked the place. Then they both turned on me and told me to shut up and keep out of it, and Tom waited for Hugh to stand up, then off they went again. It was absolutely incomprehensible, I was completely excluded, and just dithered in the hall.

There was a crash in the bedroom, my bedside table and my new reading lamp. I reckoned that was the limit. I went in tensed up to throw myself between them if needs be, and found them both sitting on the floor beside the bed, looking sheepishly at my broken lamp and Hugh handing the whiskey bottle to Tom.

'Sorry about that, love' said Hugh. 'Just playing the silly buggers, a bit pissed, won't do it again. Cheers!' He waved the whiskey bottle at me and I went over and took a swig.

I was totally bewildered. Hugh chatted away about Frankfurt whores and air hostesses as he got dressed, offered the bottle around again, and then left, shaking Tom firmly by the hand as he was going, and telling me with great formality that I was lucky to have such a fine friend.

Tom and I didn't really sleep at all that night. Jane and

David arrived back as we were clearing up and Jane, who thrives on crises, wanted a full account of the drama, so we had coffee in the sitting room and gave her her moneysworth.

Tom told her that she should get a chain put on the front door, not because of Hugh (he seemed to think Hugh was just a harmless looney – probably quite right) but because it could have been someone I didn't know. Jane agreed straightaway, and made David promise to do it the next day. She adores Tomás for some reason, and thinks I should have stuck with him right from the start and settled down to raise children in splendid rural isolation on the Beara. She has very romantic ideas about West Cork and children.

Tom had to leave next morning, ironically on the 9.50 flight. We made love, beautifully as usual – why the hell is it so special with Tom? Of course I tried to get him to stay longer but it was no use. And he wasn't just being stubborn as he usually is. I think he really would have liked to stay longer but he was already two days late. The rudder had been damaged on the crossing. That was why he'd left the boat at Falmouth instead of Lymington, and he was worried about old Pat, who was looking after his sheep back in Bethlehem, and he said it wasn't fair on old Pat to get back any later, and I couldn't argue with that.

We spent a lot of time catching up on what's been happening since I last went home. Aunt Kate never tells me enough about Tom, even though she's very good with the rest of the news. She'd probably have made a far better journalist than I ever will. Tom's really fed up with the farm. The sheep are far more difficult to look after than he imagined, and they're also far less profitable. But, typical of his luck, the land has increased enormously in value over the last few years, so he wants to sell the whole thing, and buy a pub instead. Hannah Sullivan has died, and he thinks he could do great things with the Sullivan place. It comes up for auction in January.

I can't get excited about the idea of owning a pub. Just about every other person I know in Cork seems to have this dream of running a little bar somewhere nice down west and living the quiet life. And a lot of the best people try it too, and either get totally sodden or else come running back to the city after a couple of years looking for a way of proving to themselves that they're still alive. The west is not an easy place to live, it gets melancholy, and when you're sitting on top of the means to drown your sorrows all day long the risk is too great. I'd say Tom's not immune to the west. He's only been there three years and up to now he's been kept busy with the boat and the farm, especially the farm, and without that I could easily see him getting very fond of the hard stuff.

So we had the usual old rows about him not taking himself seriously enough and me not being ready to leave London. But what I'd forgotten in the time we've been apart is how much Tom makes me laugh. He had me in stitches with a story about his girlfriend from the Dursey, the mountainy woman he calls her, he was so funny about it that I couldn't feel jealous. Anyway, as he still points out, if I want him to myself I only have to stay there with him.

In fact we ended up in the same old argument about why don't I go over and live with him, I think we were both surprised to find that it was still possible to argue about it. I thought we'd agreed ages ago that it was out of the question. Tom seems to think that I only have to grow up a bit and then I'll come to my senses and realize that its a damn good offer he's making me. He even suggested that I go back with him that very morning on the 9.50 flight.

In retrospect it infuriates me that he can disappear for over a year without even writing or phoning and then turn up and assume that I'd be prepared to drop everything and go with him. But at the time I didn't see it like that, I just felt very flattered that he still wanted me. Now I can see that it's also bloody insulting (as Digger would put it) for him to act as if my life in London didn't exist. No, it's more as if he automatically gives second-rate status to anything which has to do with me in London. I'm even beginning to suspect that he would probably have thrown Hugh out whether I wanted him to or not! He just can't understand what I like about London. He believes in how much I love the sea because he's seen that, and he knows how much Castletownbere means to me, so he assumes that if all that is the real me, then the part of me that likes London must be the false me. And the scorn that he has, well, not scorn, just the teasing I get – blackguarding, he calls it – when I start to go on about how much I enjoy earning my own living, it's all out of proportion. He over-reacts. Okay, it must look pretty laughable to him, but he's just one of those people who are good at making money. I know he's done very well for himself and all that, and he must have worked damn hard at his business in Cork to be able to sell it so soon and buy the farm. But Tom's a person who could do a lot more than simply make money, making money doesn't stretch him enough. Sometimes I really wish he was broke like me, but if he was he'd never stay that way for long, or he wouldn't be Tomás.

Anyway, we eventually fell into a sort of doze. I really like being in bed with Tom because he's so cuddly, not like all the skinny trendies I land myself with in London. He's not fat, just chunky and solid, and absolute bliss to doze with. He got me up at seven to cook him some breakfast. It hadn't occurred to me, but of course he hadn't had a proper meal for days. Luckily we had some eggs in, and I sliced up some spam and fried it and opened a tin of baked beans. What heights of gastronomic wonders! Actually I was a bit ashamed because Tom has made me so many superb breakfasts on the *Pico*.

A very strange thing happened while I was cooking breakfast. Tom had a bath, and he was getting dressed in my bedroom when I went to ask him how many eggs he wanted. He was singing to himself a bit absent-mindedly, the way he always does when he gets up early, to keep himself in a good mood, but what really stunned me was that he was singing 'The West Coast of Clare', but he'd changed Clare to Clear. He has the most lovely voice, especially when he's singing quietly and unaccompanied, and I just said something like 'Oh, I love that song' – I couldn't explain then about the reggae and having only just discovered 'Planxty' that very same evening. And Tom said *he* likes it because it reminds him of our time on Cape Clear, and didn't I know he was just a big sentimental slob, plague of my life, etc., etc.

It's only two summers ago, that visit to Clear. I remember the heatwave, and walking to the public phone box, which is bang in the middle of the island (we reckoned they put it there to make it equally inconvenient for everyone because it's miles from any other cottages) and phoning Castletownbere and Kinsale and telling everyone we were becalmed on Clear and then spending hours on board making love and missing nearly all the sunshine. Honestly, it seems like two other people in their wild irresponsible youth, not me and Tom less than two years ago. It makes me laugh to think we have such a romantic past!

I'd been planning to go over to Castletownbere to stay with Kate for a few days before Christmas on about the 20th, but after a bit of persuasion from Tom I realised that if I missed some Fleet Street office parties I could in fact get away by the 12th, less than two weeks' time now. Suddenly I feel I'd rather be there than here, and in a way it's got nothing to do with Tom at all. He says he'll meet me at Cork airport, and take me straight down to Castletown Berehaven so I can avoid Kinsale and all the Cork relations until Christmas itself.

He left soon after 7.30 and I felt really envious and stupid watching him walking down the steps and thinking I could be going with him to Heathrow and the 9.50 flight to Cork where he'd pick up his lovely old MGB and zoom down to Castletown Berehaven in time for lunch and high tide.

Oh, sod it, here I am in London being a big fucking bigshot and so fucking what.

And the bastard left his báneen socks hanging in the bathroom dripping wet and they're still not dry a whole week later and everytime I go in there and see them I think of *him* and I have to wonder how the hell and if ever we're going to work something out.

Sorrow and sadness bitterness grief
Memories I have of you
Wont leave me in peace
My mind is running back
To the west coast of Clear
Thinking of you
And the times we had there

DEVELOPMENT

The objects as well as the limits of this work will
not permit our accompanying the tourist to the west of
Glengarriff. And yet we can assure him, that it is a
goodly country to behold; one rich in wild and romantic
beauty, and abounding in objects of stirring interest. We
may in particular, point out to him from the summit of our
Pisgah, the wide spread range of the *Caha* mountains, in
the vicinity of Glengarriff; far within whose deep recesses may
be found in admirable combinations, many of those
picturesquely characteristic features, in which this whole
locality is so abundant. Of small lakes and tarns, the
number alone is marvellous; the peasantry indeed have limited
them to the number of days in the year; every mountain
summit and hollow containing one of those Alpine reservoirs.
Amongst these, *Glanmore* (i.e. the great valley) containing
within its profound depth, a fair and lonely lake, is
worth the labour of a visit. Then extending our range, we
would recommend a closer acquaintance with *Deadhe* or
Hungry-hill, than our distant prospect of it, in a preceding
page would permit; after which may be visited the farthest
western town on these shores – *Castletown-Berehaven*. Near it
are the wretched ruins of *Dunboy*, the stronghold of
O'Sullivan Bere, the history of whose siege and capture are
so amply detailed by Carew, in the pages of his 'Pacata
Hibernia'. And in the same vicinity are the prosperous
Allihies mines, the property of J. L. Puxley Esq. which give
employment to nearly one thousand persons, diffusing
abundance and comfort over an otherwise sterile and
unproductive district.

Windele's South of Ireland, Cork 1849

It was the first time she could ever remember having been happy to get back to London. The untidy urban landscape which she watched through the windows of the tube was coated in patches with hoar frost. She looked with relief at the proliferation of buildings and roads, the endless variety of cars and people, the blessed anonymity of it all. A city full of strangers.

Some of the Kinsale sailing crowd, coming over for the boat show, were on the same flight, and had offered her a ride into town in their taxi. She lied and told them her flat was right next to the tube and that she'd get home quicker that way. Other people on the Cork flight melted away between customs and the tube station, and she was able to board the train entirely unobserved. She even tore off the Aer Lingus baggage tag from her case so that no one would know where she'd come from. She wanted to be just another city face: identity, occupation, nationality and status to be idly guessed at by the more curious among her fellow travellers.

As she stepped out of South Ken station she was able to hail a passing taxi immediately. He screeched to a halt at her feet and Alex laughed at the driver through sheer exhilaration and joked, 'Hey! Just like in the movies!'

On the front-door step she realised that she'd packed her key in her suitcase so she rang the bell, hoping that Jane would be in. She was, and they greeted each other with unusual effusiveness.

Jane was radiating happiness. She'd fallen in love, he'd bought her a cooker, this was different and special, she'd had her hair softly permed, they were going to the Virgin Islands next week, her parents had given her a coffee percolator and she'd decided to leave her job at the gallery and start dealing independently.

The flat was chaotic. Jane had started to paint the sitting room as she'd need it to show pictures to clients, and Martin, the wonderful new man, had stopped her midway and insisted that she got someone in to do the job for her. No one could start before Tuesday because of the New Year holiday, so meanwhile the record player, records and books were piled up in the hall and the rest of the furniture was under dust-sheets in the middle of the room.

Alex went into raptures at the sight of the beautiful new gas cooker with an eye-level grill and automatic sparking system. The percolator gently filled the kitchen with a coffee aroma and Jane and Alex sat at the table both reflecting on the changes that a mere few weeks can make to a life.

Alex suggested adding a suspicion of Bushmills from her duty free to the coffee and Jane agreed out of curiosity. Alex would afterwards look back affectionately on this occasion, which extended well into the afternoon when she retired to bed pleading jet lag. It marked the moment when, after nearly two years of mutual reserve and wariness, she and Jane finally started getting to know each other.

First they talked about Jane and the wonderful Martin. He was a forty-six-year-old American oil man, rich, twice divorced, and commuting between London, Aberdeen and the Middle East working as some kind of consultant on oil finance. He was also, of course, an art lover. She had met him in circumstances which she described as 'absolutely Barbara Cartland'. He had come into the gallery to ask about a picture, and came back three times on the same day, each time with a flimsier pretext, until he finally suggested that she would perhaps care to continue explaining the merits of the artist over a cocktail. She did, and then, as she said with heavy irony diluting her usual coyness, they realized that they had fallen madly in love.

Martin was putting up a small amount of capital to enable Jane to start buying and selling pictures. Her own preference had always been for Victorian watercolours which she had been dealing in on the side for the last few years. There was little doubt that, given this kind of start, she would do well at it.

Martin was looking for a house outside London within easy reach of Heathrow. He wanted to remarry, and so did Jane. She was planning to keep the London flat as a pied à terre cum informal gallery, and straightaway made it clear to Alex that having Alex as a tenant was part of her plan. That way the place would be kept warm, and what's more, Jane added, dropping the pose of reassuring magnanimity and looking a bit shifty, it would mean less risk of burglary and someone to answer the phone. Alex spotted an oil finance consultant lurking behind the apparent generosity and, much to Jane's amusement, said so, thus breaking yet another bit of the ice.

Alex was grateful for Jane's frankness, and as she said to Jane, it was refreshing to hear a good luck story for a change. It confirmed the elation that she'd felt on the way in from Heathrow, an elation that came from her belief that one of the few good things about a big city like London was its endless capacity to confront its residents with new possibilities and to provide fresh scope for re-shaping a stale existence. On her good days she believed that to live in a city as grossly enormous as London should be an endless source of optimism. It was part of what she called 'the buzz'. It meant that you could never run out of new people, the way you did in Cork. The place was full of untapped pockets of potential friends, either like-minded soul-mates or some hitherto unknown variation of the human race. This was what gave its charm to those messy acres of West London which she had been staring at with such fascination as she rode in on the tube.

By the third cup of coffee they decided to drink the Black Bushmills from liqueur glasses because Jane enjoyed it so much in the coffee that she wanted to know what it tasted like alone. They allowed the percolator to perk reassuringly in the background until finally it sighed and turned itself off. Then it was Alex's turn. Jane wanted to know every detail of her stay in Cork, and especially the current state of play with 'that gorgeous hunk Tomás'. She even made an effort to pronounce his name correctly for a change – Tom-*arse*. It made Alex smile quietly.

Alex was surprised at the affection that Jane seemed to have for her, and her memory for the details that Alex had thrown out as small talk in her excitement before leaving. She wanted to be as light-hearted and good-humoured about her own story as Jane had been about hers. She wanted to reciprocate Jane's frankness, and above all she wanted Jane to understand what had happened, really to understand it, not see it as a series of gossipy clichés. But however much she wanted to let Jane know everything that had happened, she found that as she told her story she came up against vivid tableaux of emotional confusion which simply would not translate into words.

Looked at conventionally, the whole visit had been a failure from start to finish. To Alex it was not so much a failure as simply another episode in her long struggle to get to know herself better and 'work something out' with Tom. What they had worked out was that there was quite obviously no possibility of their being together in the foreseeable future.

Tom began badly by not turning up at the airport to meet Alex as he'd promised. However, he made sure that she was met by a friend of his from Cork city, who then drove her down to Castletownbere via (as Alex described it) every bloody pub in West Cork. She was fairly drunk by the time she arrived – just before closing time instead of lunchtime as expected – which partly explains the vehemence and unreasonableness of her recriminations. Tom had been tending some sick sheep every hour of the day and night for nearly three days and was not very patient with her himself.

They got over that one and the sheep recovered, allowing Alex and Tom to spend a long day in the bars of the Beara, driving out to O'Sullivan's in Allihies and over to Jacky Lynch in Eyeries, down to the Holly Bar in Ardgroom and on past the old O'Sullivan family seat at Derreen to visit Teddy and Joan's bar at Kilmakilloge before returning to Castletownbere itself to start the serious drinking. Back in familiar surroundings Alex began to slow down and get used to doing nothing very much all day.

The next problem was an Australian girl living in Dublin. She had a name, Carrie, and in any other circumstances Alex and she might have been friends. As it was, Tom had invited her to stay with him for Christmas when he met her in the summer, long before he knew Alex would be visiting her aunt Kate, and had been hoping Alex would leave for Kinsale before Carrie arrived. A man more adept at handling relationships with intelligent, contemporary women would have carried it off in one of many possible ways. It would not have been easy, but it could have been done with honesty and good humour. As it was, Tom hedged and prevaricated, kept both women in the dark as long as possible about the other's existence and made a bad decision when the crunch finally came. His idea of hospitality, especially the hospitality due to a stranger at Christmas, led him to drop Alex in favour of Carrie, even though, as he explained, Alex was the one he cared about, because Carrie was a guest in his house. It also seemed easier to him to expect Alex, as an old friend, to understand, than to try and explain the circumstances to Carrie.

Naturally Alex was outraged and bewildered, and while doing her best to keep a cheerful face on for the benefit of her aunt Kate, spent the most miserable time she could ever remember, sulking by day while pretending to read, and trying to appear her normal self while drinking in Shanahan's every evening. Tom at least had the consideration to take Carrie to The Oyster where Alex never drunk.

She went up to Kinsale with her aunt earlier than originally planned to spend the holiday with her parents in their house there. They had sold her grandmother's lovely run-down Georgian town house and built a modern ranch-style home on a plot of land overlooking the spectacular harbour. Alex totally disapproved of such sensible unsentimental behaviour on their part and referred to the comfortable place they had built for their retirement as 'the parental bungalow', a term she had coined during an argument with an Irish American she'd met on the Beara in pursuit of his 'ancestral home'. As a rule she seldom stayed there if she could possibly avoid it, preferring the uneventful, aimless life she led at aunt Kate's place to the more lively social scene in Kinsale.

For once, however, she was glad of the distractions to be found in Kinsale. She became wildly sociable, attending dinner dances at local hotels, functions at the Yacht Club, crewing for yacht races, and spending a lot of time in the latest fashionable bar in town with her cousins and a very attractive architect friend of theirs from Dublin.

She went into great detail when telling Jane about Kinsale. Alex characterised the place for Jane by the local joke which always cropped up there when meeting new people in bars: 'Are you married or do you come from Kinsale?' Jane, not being used to that way of thinking, took a long time to catch on, but once she did, she made it plain that Kinsale was a place that she wanted to hear a lot more about.

So Alex went on to describe the architect in terms that had Jane sighing approval. And at one level she was quite pleased with herself. The architect had lived in San Francisco, so as Irishmen go he was a better than average lover. And their affair had the extra edge that comes from maintaining a respectable front as Alex had to get back to her parents' house before dawn and also observe small-town etiquette and avoid being seen entering or leaving his hotel room. Moreover, the ease with which she had acquired such an urbane good-looking lover both restored her self-respect and increased her popularity locally. Tom had never been liked by the essentially rather conservative crowd of young marrieds that Alex hung around with in Kinsale, so her liaison with him and her long-standing preference for the elusive charms of Castletownbere had earned her a reputation as a bit of an eccentric.

What she didn't tell Jane about in any detail was her final visit to Castletownbere. Her parents had heavy colds and it was Alex's obvious duty to drive her aunt back home. Aunt Kate was immune to the pleasures of Kinsale and never liked to stay longer than she had to, an attitude she usually shared with her niece.

They both enjoyed the two-hour drive through roads even more deserted than normally and the mildness of the weather gave them plenty of scope for small talk. Alex and her aunt seldom had proper conversations about anything. Their intimacy was based initially on Kate's decisive backing of Alex during certain adolescent skirmishes with her parents, and thereafter maintained by letters. When they were together they had enough understanding of each other's natural reserve not to discuss anything personal. Alex had a great respect for Kate's opinions, most of which could be summed up as 'homespun philosophy' and would easily be dismissed as commonplace by someone less well-disposed than Alex.

Kate within the family was a taciturn figure who gave outsiders the impression of being difficult to get along with. She and Alex's mother kept up a constant low-key bickering about everything, and were as different as two sisters could possibly be. Kate was the elder by twelve years, had married a lawyer at eighteen and never had children of her own, nor worked at a job outside the home. Alex's mother had made a great effort to achieve both these things in moderation, and to get away from the narrow horizons which she felt Cork to offer. Kate was widowed at forty soon after Alex's parents' wedding, and had stayed on alone in Castletownbere, obstinate to all efforts by the rest of the family to get her back to Cork or Kinsale. But in Castletownbere Kate – or Mrs O'Connell as she was known by even her closest friends – was a well-loved and respected figure. She'd made friends with all the local children and had seen so many generations grow up that she was a mine of information on everyone in the area. She spent her days in a series of long good-natured chats with people she came across on her walks, her shopping trips, her card-playing evenings and her visits to the church. The older ones, of her own generation, made a point of dropping in on her from time to time for a cup of tea, knowing that Mrs O'Connell enjoyed the bit of company.

As soon as Alex parked the car outside Kate's house in the main square of Castletownbere an informal welcoming committee of passers-by gathered, and Kate stayed on the street chatting away about her Christmas while Alex (Mrs O'Connell's niece, as she was known) unpacked the car.

Alex was keen to be out of Castletownbere as fast as possible, but could not leave without ensuring that Kate, who had become increasingly frail over the last two winters, had a good fire in the sitting room and all the groceries that she needed. It was while she was waiting for Kathleen Shanahan to make up the grocery list that Jimmy and Sean came in and called a glass of Murphy's for her in the back bar. She joined them there, and by the time that her box was ready for her in the front shop, the other half was waiting for her again in the back bar. She felt duty bound to complete the round, so she hurried over to Kate's house with the box, and back to Shanahan's in time for her shout. But Jimmy and Sean had not been as guileless as they seemed, because when she got back they had disappeared and Tom was sitting in their place.

At first they didn't talk at all. He looked haggard. Alex was mesmerised, catatonic. Though she knew the sensible thing would be to walk out of the bar and leave him there she couldn't. And, though she wanted to talk, she didn't know where to start. There was too much unsaid between them.

Tom had three glasses of Bushmills to Alex's one, then broke the silence by suggesting very formally that they might go for a walk together. Alex agreed, as it seemed the best way to talk without being overheard. They took the road out of town towards Dunboy Castle, still in silence.

As they left the houses behind them, Alex looked at Tom and saw that he was silently crying. That set her off as well and they stopped in the middle of the road and embraced until Alex had to beg Tom to release her to catch her breath from his bear hug. The shock of the unexpected meeting was finally passing. They began to talk in their usual strange mixture of mutual scolding and affection. Tom said he'd been depressed and drunk ever since she'd left. Carrie had got fed up with his company and gone off to Dingle on St Stephen's Day to hear some traditional music which was, she said, the only reason she'd come west in the first place.

So then Tom had driven up to Kinsale looking for Alex and turned back at Bandon where he'd stopped for a drink and heard from some mutual acquaintance, in true small town style, about Alex and the architect. He assumed that Alex had done that to get even with him for Carrie, and asked if they could now call it quits and 'stop all this nonsense'.

Alex went cold when she heard that, and quickly lost her melting emotional state. She had never for one moment thought of revenge for Carrie, it was an impossible way to think, and showed up the great gulf between her way of being and Tom's. Anyone who thought in those terms was impossible, and the only way back to sanity was not to care, to look on him as her Kinsale friends did, as a cranky womanizer, an eccentric and a hopeless case.

But once she'd realised that she was no longer emotionally involved with Tom she could feel fond of him again, an affection which she demonstrated by hugging him and calling him all the names that she had in her mind for him. Tom seemed to experience a similar kind of relief, though his main accusation was that Alex was totally mad. One day she'd see sense and come back to him. And he hinted at a grand plan which he had thought up to tempt her back. She would hear about it, he said, from her aunt Kate in a few weeks' time, it was something he was doing especially for her.

Alex could easily guess what that was, but it didn't matter to her at all. Once she realised that her passion for Tom had burnt itself out yet again, a great weight lifted. When they reached the gates of Dunboy Castle she had a sharp flash of longing to be back in London, forging ahead with her own life and building on the reality of how she lived there.

She and Tom walked back into town holding hands, swinging their arms between them and slagging each other off in their usual style. Then she took Tom for tea with Kate and they all chatted away with great animation about nothing in particular. Alex waved goodbye to Tom and Kate with a huge smile which was largely the result of her own surprise at how rapidly her mood could change from leaden morose to light-hearted bubbling. She drove back to Kinsale in top Fangio form, with RTE2 at full volume, thrashing her father's Rover around the bends before Glengarriff and up to a hundred on the one straight stretch outside Bandon.

Once back at the parental bungalow she headed straight for the telephone and booked herself on the morning flight. She packed in three minutes and then went out on the town for a final fling with the smoothie Dublin architect. She was not particularly surprised when he announced, after an elaborate meal at the best restaurant in town, that he was actually very happily married to an American who had taken the children home for Christmas. She had half suspected something like that all along, and was more annoyed with her cousins who'd introduced them, than with the architect.

Jane explained that architects were to be avoided on principle, they were all screwed up because they were neither *real* professionals nor *real* artists. Alex said she knew one thing they *really* were, and they both shouted drunkenly: *real* bastards.

Castletownbere,
Co. Cork

Monday

My Dear Alex,
Many thanks for your letter. I always enjoy hearing from you.

I was glad to have the news of your safe journey that you left at Shanahan's. I had not time to put the candles up before your flight, but I lit some for you as soon as I heard you'd arrived.

It's nice to hear that you have lots of work to do. Imagine getting paid to eat in restaurants. Isn't it grand to be in demand. I was glad of the copies that you left me here because then I had something to show to your auntie Maíre. They were down on the Saturday for the Xmas visit and we went to lunch in Glengarriff to Doc Ryan's. It was the only place open this time of year apart from the Dutch place and we'd never eat there. They were asking for you. They didn't know you were over at all, you'd think they would have heard by now. It makes me think that no one visits at all in the city if they have to come down here to learn the news. And then they tell me I should move up to the city to be less on my own, there's no sense in them at all.

It rained all day yesterday and I couldn't go to devotions at four it was too dark but please God I can make it up on Friday. This is a desperate time of year with nothing but rain and long evenings and nothing at all to talk about. I don't know how you would like it if you had to live here all the year round, but as you're so young and lively I'm sure you'd find a way.

That reminds me. Your friend Thomas O'Sullivan bought Hannah Sullivan's bar in the end. They say he paid a fortune for it and they tell me he is calling it the Berehaven Inn and he will be doing 'pub grub' of all things. He sold the farm to a Dutchman and they say he's wanting to build a motel in Bethlehem. Whatever next I say, 'The Motel Bethlehem', there's the Dutch for you. Thomas was asking after you and said to be sure to give you the news if I was writing. He is a lovely man and I'm delighted with my new neighbour.

That's all for now.

Love from your

Auntie Kate

*   *   *

53

'SHIT!'

'What's that, your Barclaycard bill?' asked Jane, full of sympathy.

'No,' said Alex sighing. 'Just a letter from my aunt in Castletown Berehaven.'

Alex had noticed that since getting back to London she'd taken advantage of every possible opportunity (like someone suffering from a teenage crush) to say the long name, 'Castletown Berehaven', where she could simply have said 'Castletownbere' or 'The Beara' or 'county Cork' or 'Ireland' or even nothing at all.

It didn't make much sense to her either.

*　　*　　*

Their flat was midway between King's Road and the river, about five minutes' walk from both. It was on the unfashionable side of an unfashionable square, the side that never got sunlight through the front windows. It was not a cheerful flat in winter.

Alex's room was at the back and looked down on to a basement patio which was surrounded on all sides by extensions which had been built haphazardly on to the mid-Victorian houses to accommodate bathrooms and sculleries. Alex had a kind of French window opening on to a small metal balcony. In high summer it got the evening sun, but it was too dirty to sit out on because the back area was infested by pigeons. The council had once put down some foul sticky repellent but the pigeons no longer took any notice of it, so there was now a combination of birdshit, sticky repellent, and the flea-ridden birds themselves. Alex liked their subdued cooing and fluttering. Sometimes, after checking that none of the neighbours were watching, she put old pieces of bread out on her balcony for them.

Alex was not a person who liked routine. But, since moving

to Jane's, her Sundays started to acquire something of a regular pattern.

In the weeks after her return from Castletownbere Jane and Martin were usually away, staying at Martin's new place in the country, so Alex got used to having the flat to herself at weekends. If she woke up in time she wandered over to the eleven o'clock sung mass. But more often she didn't get out of bed till after midday. Then she cooked a brunch of eggs scrambled in a frying pan in lots of butter with tomatoes, cheese, ham, green peppers – whatever she found in the fridge – thrown in with them. She ate her eggs in the sitting room with toast and lots of fresh coffee while she read the Sunday papers and listened to appropriate waking up music – usually American rock.

She forced herself to turn over all the pages of the news section of the *Sunday Times* first although she seldom read any item in full. She rewarded herself for that feat of self-discipline by flicking through Jane's *Sunday Express*, concentrating on the gossip column and its editorial page. She enjoyed the perverse sense of horror which its outrageously reactionary opinions never failed to provide. After that she went back to the *Times* and scanned the book reviews diligently, ending up by checking the TV page to see if there was anything she wanted to watch in the evening.

After the papers it was time for her walk. She had two to choose from and she thought of them as the sociable walk and the unsociable walk. The sociable walk took her across King's Road, up to South Kensington then up Exhibition Road past the Science Museum and the side entrance to the Victoria and Albert Museum to Kensington Gardens. Here she walked in a big circle which took her past one side of the Albert Memorial, up to the Serpentine, down past Peter Pan, up to the Round Pond, down to the squirrels in the flower garden and out again almost where she'd begun, on the opposite side of the Albert Memorial.

At the end of this walk she dropped in for tea at her parents'. They still had the same flat she'd grown up in, on the sixth floor of a solid Victorian block of flats near the Albert Hall. She liked the warmth and solidity of the block, the firm polished wood banisters, the red Turkey carpet, the brass door knobs, the heavy clanking lift gate and the well-worn buttons in the lift. The self-confidence and stuffy solidity of the place, which had oppressed and stifled her to the point of hysteria as a teenager, now soothed and reassured her.

It was the same with her parents – the predictable surprise with which they greeted her, the good-humoured clichés which once would have irritated her beyond endurance and led her to make thoughtlessly sarcastic replies, she now handled calmly by employing a kind of exaggerated mock outrage, which was what her parents had come to expect of her.

They drank Earl Grey tea together and ate chocolate digestive biscuits while Alex was entertained with stories about the small events of her parents' quiet social life and bits of family news from Cork. They never spoke to her about their work unless she pushed them. Both her parents were nearing retirement age. Her mother, a neat elegant woman, now worked only part-time and, although both her parents had reasonably distinguished medical careers, they were looking forward to the prospect of unlimited idleness which they hoped lay ahead of them.

After tea, dry sherry was offered, and Alex always accepted one glass before setting off to walk home. Her decision to walk always involved a ritual of her father offering a lift, her mother giving warnings about muggings and Alex's curt reassurances. She had a horror of being fussed over, and her parents seemed to possess the gift of creating a massive fuss out of absolutely nothing. She usually spent the entire half-hour it took her to walk home recovering from the fuss.

Her other walk, the unsociable one, was shorter and in many ways more enjoyable. She walked from the flat down to the river and then in a rectangle which took her along the embankment of the Thames to Albert Bridge, over the river at the bridge, down the opposite embankment path which was in Battersea Park to Chelsea Bridge, and back across the river to Chelsea Embankment.

It was visually a very striking walk. Her favourite view was at the start of the walk as she went up the embankment to Albert Bridge. Through the pretty curves of the suspension bridge she could look at the sun already starting to set behind the distant grey shapes of Lots Road power station. Sometimes the light bulbs on the girders of Albert Bridge were lit by the time she reached Chelsea Bridge, and she could stand and stare back at the other frivolously-decorated bridge superimposed on a grandiloquent 'sunset over power station'. She did quite a lot of thinking on her unsociable walk, and often crossed the bridges twice in order to follow up a particular train of thought.

She liked the unsociable walk for other reasons too. The most simple one was that she encountered fewer families than in Kensington Gardens, and fewer couples. There seemed to be more solitary walkers, alone or with a dog, and so she felt less conspicuous. The other important reason was that Chelsea Embankment and Battersea Park held none of the memories and associations with her childhood that Kensington did. On the Kensington walk she was confronted by stale memories of fixed moments in her life between the ages of five and eighteen which she found annoying, but not quite annoying enough to stop her entirely from taking that walk.

All that she associated with the Battersea walk was the time that she'd spent living in Jane's flat. She saw that as a positive time, a period in her life when she'd started learning to come to terms with herself and to know herself through being alone. Childhood and adolescence had been a series of rebellions and pointless struggles with nannies, parents, teachers. . . .

University and her postgraduate work had taken on a manic quality in retrospect, as if she had put an immense amount of energy into doing a lot of not really necessary things. That wasn't helped by her subsequent passive absorption in Henry, an absorption resulting almost in self-annihilation. Moving in with Jane and working as a journalist instead of going to Ireland and living with Tom marked, to Alex's mind, the lamentably late start of a self-determining life.

In the weeks following her Christmas visit to Castletown-bere she tended to take the Battersea walk rather than the Kensington one. She even found herself setting off for the Battersea walk on weekdays in total darkness after she'd packed up work.

Her work was starting to attract attention. She enjoyed writing, seeing it as a craft in which she was a mere beginner, learning something new about technique with each job she tackled. She became totally involved in whatever project she was working on.

She was now doing some book reviewing and occasional

interviews with authors, and being very conscientious about it. As a result it occupied a disproportionate amount of her time relative to what she was paid. But she'd also had a lucky break through John, her guide book friend, and was helping him to update a flashy restaurant guide which he produced for distribution to passengers arriving in London on a certain airline. The work was ludicrously well paid, considering how enjoyable it was, and as it meant eating out at least once a day, she was spending no money at all on food. But it did mean that she was quite literally working night and day, and so her Battersea walk had come to be very important as a break when she could indulge in the luxury of thinking about herself. That was something she had previously only done by writing copious journals. There was no time anymore for unpaid writing.

She was pleased with her work, and the neat sums of money which were now accumulating in her deposit account pleased her too. While she had no plans for using the money beyond the relatively minor expense of buying some new clothes and a few records, she enjoyed the knowledge that she was able to earn enough money to live above subsistence level. She had always been cautious about money: not mean exactly, but operating in the same way that she had been taught to navigate a boat – when in doubt about your exact position, always assume yourself to be in the worst possible one. Being vague by nature, and not mathematically inclined, she was unsure about how much money she was earning. As long as the bills got paid with a bit left over she reckoned she was doing all right.

She sometimes worried a little about what would happen to her if Jane decided to sell the flat once she was married to Martin, but one thing that Alex was quite self-controlled about was not worrying unnecessarily before the event. So rather than thinking about what she would do if she was forced to move flats she preferred to daydream about buying herself a car. A convertible sports car, she reckoned, red or maybe dark green, an MGB or a Spitfire, or maybe one of those little Italian ones with pop-up headlamps, but in that case why not a TR7? She didn't have much idea of prices and things. It was only a daydream after all.

She thought about the men she knew quite often too. Not Tomás, he was totally remote to her normal consciousness.

Tomás was only there in the moments between waking and sleeping when she smiled dozily and, planning a seduction, stretched out a foot to tease his, searched with an arm for his big solid back, then jolted awake to curse the tricks the mind plays on the half-waking.

The present was nice enough, so nice that Alex often ironically raised her eyebrows to heaven in thankful surprise. Apart from having interesting work, an increasingly happy if precarious living arrangement at Jane's and a surplus of money, there were plenty of men around too.

Alex had got into the habit of thinking of her life as three potential disaster areas – work and money, then home base, family and friends, and finally sex, lovers and love affairs. If things were bad in all three simultaneously she would, she believed, have genuine grounds for being miserable. But as it happened things were usually okay in one, if not two, of the areas. At the moment, if she forgot her recent skirmish with Tomás, she was in that rare state where things appeared to be okay in all three areas at the same time.

She was still seeing both Digger and Andy, neither of whom she thought of as the usual sort of affair. She was beginning to think that affairs, like families, are usually extraordinary set-ups far removed from the normal image. Andy O'Sullivan (no relation to Tom), the man she most enjoyed being with at the moment, had been darting in and out of her life since she was a teenager.

Andy played guitar and harmonica, wrote catchy tunes, and claimed to hate the pop music business which his talents had inevitably thrown him into. Jane adored Andy, and at first Alex had cynically attributed this to Jane being impressed because Andy was on the point of becoming very rich and famous. Lately she'd admitted that it was perhaps a result of Andy's considerable personal charm and wonderful telephone manners, and that she was probably inheriting Andy's paranoia about new friends only wanting to know him because of his fame.

He was already causing enough of a stir within the pop music business to get mentioned in gossip columns. Recently a colleague of hers had even mentioned his 'constant companion' Alex, referring to her as 'stunning hackette Alex Buckley'. She pinned the clipping on the noticeboard above her desk and was momentarily terribly thrilled. She really felt she'd arrived, it was far more exciting than her own hard-earned by-lines. And Jane was quite touchingly impressed. Then she felt absurd to let it matter so much, and threw the cutting away without even showing it to her parents. Her parents would have been amused at it, because they knew that Alex and Andy were childhood friends, and Andy's father had been at medical school with them.

Andy and Alex had always got on well together, and he had been her very first lover. She attached no particular importance to losing her virginity, and had been glad that it happened in such a casual way with someone she liked, rather than being a further complication in some passionate love affair.

They had kept in touch over the years, either as friends or lovers depending on their mutual circumstances. They both liked the current set-up because it was reassuring (both having taken their share of knocks in recent years) to be able to make love with someone who was warm and affectionate, but could be relied on to make no further demands nor expect any commitment.

Andy's success had made him bewildered and isolated, and this time round Alex found him even more attractive than usual. He was never an easy person to be with and after the blandness of a lot of the men she met she enjoyed the demands that his cantankerous behaviour made on her patience and ingenuity. He travelled a lot, but since Christmas he and Alex had spent as much time together as their work allowed.

Alex and Andy usually stayed in his flat, which was conveniently close to hers, and listened to Beethoven (his choice) or Bach (hers) and smoked grass and drank wine. They didn't talk much about Ireland, even though Andy was buying a house in Kinsale and they had a number of mutual friends there. In fact they didn't talk much at all. Sometimes they went to a restaurant or a club, but more often they'd watch TV and, like a couple of bored teenagers, have fits of giggling at their own bad jokes about the programmes. It was very relaxing. Sometimes Andy went on shopping sprees in Harrods Food Halls and he and Alex would construct ludicrous feasts and eat them lying on the floor in front of the gas-fired log fire. Andy seemed lost, and Alex felt sorry for him. Jane thought Alex was in love with him but, as Alex explained, part of the reason that Andy felt safe with her was that she knew him far too well ever to fall in love with him.

Digger understood perfectly about Andy. He was Alex's other regular lover, also a figure from her past, whom she'd re-met unexpectedly at the party where Hugh had been so disgusted at her behaviour. She and Digger had been lovers during their first year at university some eight years previously. When Alex missed a period during the end of year exams she and Digger faced up bravely to the possibility that she was pregnant and Digger most gallantly offered to marry and support her. He took her to a place near Nottingham to meet his father, a wealthy widowed barrister living with his mistress in a Victorian mock castle with a miniature railway in the grounds, and she thought maybe it wouldn't be so bad to become part of such a comfortable eccentric English family. Then she had a period, and she and Digger gratefully disengaged themselves and began fighting over anything and everything, and separated for the summer vac. Digger dropped out of university and spent a year in the States. He returned a committed socialist and moved to another university to study politics. Digger was now working as an adviser to a politician.

Alex still found Digger attractive, even though his very prosaic mind and clichéed outlook often annoyed her. At times he seemed so much a typical product of his upbringing and subsequent predictable rebellion that it was hard to see him as an individual at all. All his attitudes seemed to be formed by stereotyped thought about reported events rather than his own experience of things. This was partly what made it possible to have an affair with him in which there was no sentimental exploitation nor jealousy. He had decided that this was the civilised way to handle sex. They were completely frank about other people in their lives, and each knew that the other would one day be gloriously swept off their feet and back into romantic clichés by someone more easily compatible.

Besides Digger and Andy, Alex managed to keep in touch with a wide circle of other friends and was enjoying a series of long chats with Jane. It was all, she kept telling herself, extremely pleasant. But while she walked briskly over one bridge and then back across the other her face would often end up in a puzzled frown. In spite of all three areas of her life being perfectly okay she was constantly brought up against the sensation of living in a transition. It had nothing to do with not being in love with anyone, it went far deeper than that and was far more existentially disturbing. It was not the same as drifting. She already felt that she was tying up loose ends, completing circles, preparatory to moving on, but as yet she had no intention of moving anywhere, nor changing her life in any way at all.

*   *   *

Andy turned the gas-fired logs up to maximum and refilled Alex's glass from the bottle of claret that was standing in the grate. Then he lay down again on the floor cushions and shuffled through an axis of heels, arse and elbows in an effort to get comfortable.

'Jeez, I'd like to strangle the woman who did this flat. How can you have a fireplace like this and no sofa in front of it?'

Andy's dislike of his current landlady – the term was his deliberately misleading way of describing the formidably elegant woman who had momentarily cornered the market in rental of grossly over-decorated apartments to the rich – was one of his main topics of conversation. It was usually followed, as now, by some remark about his plans for his own place in Kinsale: 'I'm having two leather Chesterfields and a decent bit of Persian carpet, none of this shabbytat rubbish.'

Alex had not yet relaxed sufficiently after a very tense working day to avoid the temptation to argue.

'God, I'd have thought you could do a bit better than that! *Everyone* has bloody Chesterfields, even Jane. And if they're leather you're forever sliding off them. I'd have one of those big old-fashioned chintzy things with feather cushions that you just disappear in.' She squirmed a bit on her floor cushion and sat up on an elbow to look for her glass. 'But I must say I agree these things are bloody awful.'

She didn't want to fight with Andy, she was feeling sorry for him again. He'd just finished recording a new record and had ten days almost free of commitments before he and his band began a UK tour to promote the album, and he was obviously having trouble filling in his time. He'd phoned Alex at three in the afternoon to ask her out to lunch and had been surprised and apologetic to find her hard at work to meet a six o'clock deadline. She'd come straight over after that, and found him on his floor cushions surrounded by the week's music papers with the claret and glasses warming in the grate. She thought it was 'sweet' that he had not started drinking before she arrived. It also said something to her about his uneasiness with his apparently glamorous lifestyle.

They had been looking through the cinema pages of the evening paper and could find nothing exciting enough to make them want to leave the warmth of Andy's flat and face the unusually cold night outside. They were now supposed to be trying to think of a restaurant instead. Alex had been about to suggest a Thai place where everyone sat on cushions on the floor when Andy had made the remarks about his own floor cushions, so there was obviously no longer any point in mentioning that. But Andy, as he lay staring at the beamed ceiling, was also thinking.

'What about the new place in Covent Garden?'

'Ziggy's?'

'Yeah, the new one.'

'It's terrible. I had lunch there last week and it was absolutely dreadful. I had to cover it for John's guide thing and I told him to leave it out.'

'Jeez, I'd forgotten about the guide thing, you must be sick of restaurants.' Then he added peevishly, 'Why don't we stay in again, how's that for a great idea?'

'I don't mind, Andy, honestly. Whatever you feel like. . . .'

He picked up her placating tone of voice immediately: '. . . "I don't mind, whatever you feel like" – jeez, woman, I thought you were the one with all the fucking bright ideas. . . .'

They both sat up and unexpectedly found that they were staring at each other. Alex tried not to look hurt, and that meant not feeling hurt. Whatever she said, she knew that it would be fatal to apologize and fatal to conciliate. Andy at the moment would not tolerate anything which felt like condescension, and mistook docility for sycophancy. The only way to handle him was to be sure he got as good as he gave. She relaxed back on to the cushions away from the pressure of his bad-tempered stare and drawled lazily, faking a stifled yawn, 'For Christsake, what's wrong with just staying in if that's what we both feel like doing? We'll open another bottle or three of wine and watch the box and cook some food, I think that's fantastic.'

'No, hang on there, woman, I've got it, fucking brilliant, wait!'

He climbed the ladder to his platform bed at a run, rummaged in a suitcase underneath the bed, and came back downstairs with a Scrabble set.

At the sight of the Scrabble set Alex's spirits soared. She lost all her calculated sensitivity to Andy as a neurotic star to be cossetted and treated with care, and saw only the old Andy that she'd known as a fellow misunderstood teenager. Scrabble had formed an important part of their adolescence as, besides being a game that they had played for hours on end as teenagers in Kinsale, it used to be their codeword and euphemism for sex. It was probably well over ten years since they'd had a proper game of Scrabble together, and was indeed an appropriate solution for the evening ahead.

Andy fetched an opium table from the other side of the room and placed it in front of the fire with the Scrabble board on it while Alex rearranged the cushions.

They were both unusually silent as the game got under way, suddenly absorbed in memories of themselves when young and the elaborately contrived personalities that they had cultivated then in order to appear interesting – their outrageous, often thoughtless behaviour and their arrogant belief in themselves as special and different from everyone around them. The memories of their past pretentiousness were almost embarrassing, but maybe, they both reflected, in a way they had been right. Maybe they had by now proved themselves to be what others would judge as 'different' – talented, unconventional, successful, *interesting*. It was certainly true in Andy's case, and in many ways Alex too was now starting to prove herself as someone 'out of the ordinary'. It was exactly the sort of future that she and Andy had dreamed of for themselves, although in vaguer and more grandiose terms. Being here didn't quite feel like the triumph it should. Once again Alex had the overwhelming sense of being in transition without knowing where she had started from nor where she was about to arrive.

Andy's thoughts ran along far less philosophical lines, being mainly a nostalgic recollection of isolated incidents until he realized that summer memories belonging to nine or ten different years had fused together. And it all seemed so long ago, like someone else and a bit of a twerp what's more.

After an hour they'd lost track of whose turn it was to play next and neither of them cared. As Andy came back from the kitchen with another bottle of claret he looked at Alex a bit mistily and opened the floodgates by saying, 'Do you know, I honestly believed I'd never live to see twenty-one?'

He took off then, a long stream of questions and memories: 'Remember Eddie and Teresa, the picnic at Lough Ine, were you there at the haymaking on Barry's farm, what about the day the Frenchman nearly drowned with the cramp in Bally-maccus and your auntie Kate sitting on the butter and Tommy Barry's stories of the IRA and the Freestaters, and Garry Bax's tent and the ghost hunt on the Fort Hill and midnight swim-ming at the paddock and rowing up to Kilmacsimon and sailing with the Hogans, the time we got becalmed, remember, remember, remember. . . .'

Alex felt as if she was being hit over the head with snippets cut from her life before it got fouled up by whatever it was that now made the past seem so simple and appealing. How easy it all was then! They argued over details and laughed and wondered why, apart from one spectacular thunderstorm, it never rained in their memories.

'Jesus,' said Andy, 'Last time I was in Kinsale it did nothing but rain the whole fucking time, and me without even a Scrabble partner.'

'Christ,' said Alex, 'I know the feeling. Everyone our age is bloody married with 3.6 kids' (or else they're crazy like Tom or Dublin smoothies like the architect, she added in her mind).

'I sometimes wonder why the hell I've bought a house there. I keep thinking, will I ever spend much time in it, or will I be screaming to get out as soon as I'm over.'

'Oh no, you'll love it once you're settled there, and you'll never stay long enough to get really fed up. As long as you can get out of the place in the winter you're okay.' Alex knew he was only asking for reassurance, but couldn't resist adding, 'But I don't know if you wouldn't have been better to go further west, Kinsale is getting polluted with bloody affluence. Now if you'd chosen somewhere like Schull or Crook or Goleen or even the Beara. . . .'

'Jesus Christ! The Beara! I don't know how you can stick it down there. And that awful dump Castletownbere –' (he pronounced the final syllable 'beer') – 'It's like the end of the bloody world, that place, it must be one of the dreariest towns in the west. Then down towards the Dursey out in the country it just gets more and more desolate. Allihies and Eyeries. I suppose that's why you like it. I've always thought you'd end up in a *tighín* on the side of some rocky hill overlooking the Atlantic wandering around barefoot in a red velvet cloak and writing bloody poems.'

'Great idea!' said Alex. 'I must get a red velvet cloak, I always knew there was something missing in my life. A red velvet cloak and a dog. A big dog, a hound . . . that reminds me, I had this incredible "flash of lucidity"' – a phrase from the philosophising phase of their adolescence – 'the other day when I was walking in Hyde Park. Do you realise . . .' she paused for effect '. . . there are probably more trees in Hyde Park than there are on the whole of the Beara Peninsula?' Another pause. 'Isn't that an amazing thought?'

Andy shrugged and said drily, 'Mind blowing.' Then, because he did on reflection find it rather amazing, he laughed and added, 'How long do you think it would take to count them? On the Beara I mean.'

'Bloody months . . . hey, what a wonderful idea! Do you think I could get a grant from the Arts Council to do it? If I convince them it's verbal minimalism, a poem, something like "Hyde Park 368 Beara 92" only it has to be based on the real number of trees to become a real poem . . . ah no, I've forgotten the old plantation at Derreen and the new soft woods at Ross Macowen, it would never work. . . .'

'You're crazy, do you know that? You'll never bloody change. Sometimes you terrify me.' He rolled over on the cushions in mock hysterics, accidentally kicking the Scrabble board over.

'Oh dear,' Alex sat up and made an effort to compose herself, 'hang on, look it's nearly half-ten, we'd better eat something sometime.'

'Ach, come here.' Andy pulled her down on to the cushions

66

again and flicked the dimmer switch at his side. There were some things the landlady had got right.

'Very bloody smooth,' said Alex.

'Jesus woman, you're so fucking romantic it's just not true.'

Alex laughed, 'Mungry.'

Another word from the past, borrowed from a B. S. Johnson novel that they'd both gone wild about during one of the summers.

'Mungry too. Let's go up to the fucking pizzas and get it over with.'

'Oh, great!'

Silly as it may have appeared, for Alex and Andy it was a cathartic sort of evening, and became very important to both of them in different ways. First of all, it re-established the kind of carefree friendship which they'd both been kidding themselves was already the basis of their renewed relationship. For Andy, Alex had been, up to that point, a convenient companion who could be relied on not to bore him by over-reacting to his new status as one of the famous, and not to embarrass him by believing in his publicity. Above all, he knew that she didn't want anything from him, not the kudos of being known as his girlfriend nor the right to live in his flat while he was away, nor useful introductions and certainly not expensive presents or money. In fact he sometimes thought she was a bit slow altogether, not stupid of course, but naïve and unaware of how best to promote herself and her interests. It was the one thing that he came close to disliking about her, her utter indifference to other people's opinion of her, and her own position in the world she worked in. Surely she could do a bit better than simply anonymously updating guide books and pamphlets and only being known by name for book reviews and in-depth interviews with writers, both of which she seemed to sweat over for a ridiculously long time.

But the Scrabble evening brought back the Alex he'd known before, to adults a withdrawn, reserved child, always buried in a book when not messing around in boats, but to her contemporaries the ringleader, the one who not only had great ideas for things to do, but also knew how to present a totally innocuous façade to their parents to cover the wildest escapades.

And the Alex who talked, who talked endlessly as they walked over rough headlands climbing through brambles to lie on empty strands or sailed to the same strands in her dilapidated dinghy or sat with her books in a private corner of someone's house, the Alex who filled his head with words and dreams inspired by Kerouac and Bob Dylan and later Hermann Hesse and Mervyn Peake then Camus and Sartre, B. S. Johnson, Flann O'Brien, her D. H. Lawrence phase until finally, at the end of the D. H. Lawrence phase, Alex went off to her English university and stopped coming to Kinsale for the summer months. For Andy those memories of Alex and that crucial period in his life before he left Cork for the pop world of Dublin and London represented something that he liked about himself, and something that he knew had helped him to succeed in his chosen career.

Andy had a long think the morning after the Scrabble as he lay in bed after Alex's early departure wondering what to do with the endless day ahead of him. He decided that Alex was not just an amiable, half-crazy but familiar person to screw, but that she was also someone to whom he owed a kind of artistic debt, someone who had been an important part of his formation and as such deserved to reap some positive benefit from his success. He knew that their present arrangement was not going to last long. He was merely marking time with her until he fell in love again or felt again sufficiently secure in himself to accept the attentions of one of his many fans, preferably a blonde one with big boobs, he thought, ignoring the hard-on which accompanied the idea. But meanwhile he'd do something nice for Alex, something which would help her to get her act together, that was the trouble with Alex, he reckoned, she needed to get her act together and a little help from a friend like himself could have a decisive effect on her future.

*   *   *

Alex read through the review one last time. She'd spent the whole day writing the two short pages, getting up at eight-thirty and settling down to her desk by nine with the phone off the hook. By midday she had a reasonable first draft typed up and ate her lunch – bread and cheese and a cup of coffee – at her desk, with the novel propped up in front of her, skimming though it again to confirm her impressions.

She took a short walk after lunch for a change of air and a think, and went up to the supermarket to buy food for the evening. Andy had left the day before on the first leg of his UK tour and Digger was coming over for dinner. It was a dull grey day, the sort of day, she thought to herself, when it's hard to believe that the freshness and renewal of spring is about to transform everything in the city. There were snowdrops in the square, but no sign as yet of the blossom which would soon make it into a gentler kind of world.

The afternoon was spent in crossings-out and re-typings, pencil chewing and searches for the exact word, a re-shuffling of paragraphs and a new running order which was almost what she wanted. By five o'clock she knew it was pointless to do any more: it must now be slept on to give the old subconscious a chance to do its work before tomorrow morning's final typing.

A writing day like this always gave her great satisfaction and the feeling that she was fully entitled to spend a frivolous evening relaxing over a few drinks, preferably in good company. Reading days, on the other hand, still left her feeling very guilty, even though reading was now part of her paid work. If she hadn't finished the novel by the evening then she kept on reading until she had. And if it had been short enough to get through in a day, then she'd start reading it again, or look at some of the earlier works, or just sit and brood over it, making ever more tortuous notes of her impressions. But the days she hated most were what she called her street days when she had to go up to Fleet Street to deliver copy or pick up a new novel or see John to deliver guide book copy and discuss future work. Her colleagues all seemed to share a pompous belief in their own importance so that even the ones whom she personally liked on neutral ground became unbearable in their work places. She was always glad not to need to become any more closely involved in their world than she already was.

She'd had almost a whole week of street days thanks to Andy and his bright idea, but as she put the review in a cardboard folder and placed the folder on top of her typewriter to rest for the night, she reflected that, much as she had complained about all the editorial meetings and self-promotion demanded of her, it would probably be worthwhile in the end.

The kitchen sink was elbow-deep in coffee cups and side plates from the last two days so, as she was by nature a tidy methodical worker, she dealt with the existing mess before creating a new one. Once the dishes were dripping dry and the onions and garlic were frying to start her spaghetti sauce, she opened the red wine, decanted it, and poured herself a glass muttering, 'Cook's privilege, cheers.' As far as she knew, it was only when cooking that she talked to herself.

As she added the mince and tomatoes and a generous drop of wine to the frying pan she heard Jane shouting hallo from the front door. She stuck her head out of the kitchen and saw Jane struggling in with a couple of paintings wrapped in blankets.

'Darling!' shouted Jane, 'You're actually *in*. I don't believe it . . . shit!' She cursed as she dropped her open handbag on to her foot and kicked its contents over the hall floor scattering Tampax in all directions in her efforts to free her foot and drag the paintings in far enough to close the front door.

'Oh, I can't bear it,' she started laughing as she stared at her face powder which had snapped open, its contents drifting across a rug. 'Here I am not even inside the front door for two seconds and the flat's a total disaster area. I don't know how you can stand it.'

It was a typical Jane-style crisis, the sort of scene she loved to create and then dramatize in a way which, until quite recently, Alex had found deeply irritating. But nowadays, whether it was due to some change in herself, or simply to the fact that she and Jane saw each other less often, she'd come to accept and even participate in Jane's chaos.

'Watch it, no . . . now you've done it,' she shouted as Jane trod in the spilt powder and spread it across the rug. 'And me expecting company for dinner, God help us.' Her impression of the scolding houseproud Cork woman always went down well on these occasions. It ended abruptly with another exclamation of 'shit', from Alex this time. The mince had stuck. She threw more wine in and scraped at the frying pan. Jane was by now leaning over her shoulder with a teaspoon, poised to take a taste, another habit that no longer annoyed her. In fact, she'd missed it recently. She turned her back to Jane and pushed the spoon away. 'Hang on, I haven't seasoned it yet, give us a bloody chance. Look, have a glass of wine, Digger's bringing another bottle.'

'Oh, Digger! How super, just like old times. Cheers!' Jane sat down at the table, throwing her empty handbag on top of some discarded onion skins, and looked up at Alex coquettishly: 'Guess what?'

'What?'

'I'm out on the razz tonight ... with David actually, yipeeee.'

Alex was rubbing a handful of oregano into her sauce and trying to move it around the pan without spilling it. 'David?' she repeated.

'I've given old fussy boots the slip. If he phones, you haven't seen me for ages. . . .'

'Well, I haven't.'

'I'm still supposed to be in Bath at the auction, but David caught me here just as I was leaving and Sara's throwing one of her parties this evening so I thought I'd sneak back a day early for the party and sod old fussy boots. . . .'

'Fussy boots? Martin?'

'God, you've no idea. He's been driving me up the bloody wall. *Everything* has to be just *so*' – she made an effort to imitate his Texan drawl. 'Everything in its place and a place for everything, hon, that's how I like my home to be run ... Farking 'ell!'

'I can imagine,' said Alex drily.

'That's it, you're made for each other, brilliant solution!'

Alex remained silent, feigning concentration on cooking.

'No, seriously,' Jane pushed her hair out of her eyes with a despairing gesture. 'It's all over. That's why I'm carrying all these Tampax around. I've been pretending to have some awful gynaecological problem for weeks to avoid sleeping with him. I can't take any more. I'm just going to behave so atrociously that he gives up.'

'Isn't that a bit drastic? I mean, he's been awfully kind to you, and I thought . . . yuch. . . .' Alex picked the onion skins off Jane's handbag and threw them in the bin.

'Well, kind, I mean with money yes, but he's got pots of it, and anyway I've worked my arse off fixing his house so I don't think he can bitch about that.' A scowl passed over her face. 'Well, he can, but it won't make a sodding bit of difference. I'm absolutely finished with him.'

'Why don't you tell him then?' Alex believed in principle in keeping her private life as simple and uncluttered as her living surroundings.

'I am telling him, aren't I?' Jane laughed again. Alex had a flashback to that terrible scene with Hugh the night she'd re-met Digger and abdicated her right to criticize. Jane burbled on with an enthusiasm that Alex hadn't seen in her for a long time. 'My God, am I going to get smashed tonight! I think I'll try and pick up a lord, I feel like a bit of class for a change, my name in William Hickey . . . Americans, yuch phooey.'

'That reminds me! You haven't heard, have you?' Alex tipped her chair back and imitated one of Jane's flirtatious poses.

'Heard what? . . . Don't tell me . . . you're engaged to Andy?' She laughed again a bit maliciously, having finally understood how remote this idea was to Alex's mind.

'No, even better, he's fixed up this trip, at least I have, with a bit of help from his manager. The band's going to the States to play for a week in some honky tonk bar and record a new live album. Andy's got heavily into country rock, and it's some crazy promotional idea. Anyway, he's given me exclusive UK coverage, so I flogged the idea to a Sunday Colour mag and we're all off on this great freebie.'

'That's amazing. It's really nice of Andy. He must be getting dead keen.'

'No way,' Alex had guessed at the none too subtle path that Andy's mind had been following. 'In fact, it would appear to be the big E on the one hand, but that was kind of inevitable. It's a relief in a way. And you'll never guess who the colour supp are sending to do the photos. . . .'

'Not Henry!' They both laughed, sharing the same slightly desperate mood.

'Thank God, no, but its a friend of his, Conor.'

Jane looked blank, so Alex elucidated.

'Christ, he's fantastic, he had an exhibition at the Contemporary about a year ago called "New Ireland", really heavy social comment stuff. . . .'

'Oh, God, the Irish mafia strikes again.'

'Oh no, he's a Dub, that's something else altogether. But he's really nice. You know how most photographers are just ego on two legs, but Con's really different, sort of quiet and miles away most of the time. But I'm not after him or anything, it's just that when you think of all the turds I could have got landed with photographically, Conor's a real stroke of luck.'

She filled their glasses again, as Jane remarked with uncharacteristic seriousness: 'God, all the men I work with are bloody gay. The women, too, come to think of it. Bath was horrible, they all know one another too, yuch.'

'Oh, I know what you mean,' said Alex sympathetically. Jane did not often talk about her work and it was all too easy to forget that she was going through a tough and lonely time, establishing herself in a new field. Alex had come to realise that the poses hid a very solid core.

'Ah well,' Jane picked up her handbag and moved towards the hall to retrieve its contents. 'To work, to work. I am going to look so bloody glamorous this evening. You'd better pee now if you want to because I'm going to hog the bathroom for yonks.'

Digger was late, Alex thought, but then couldn't remember if she'd told him to arrive at any particular time. She was lying on the sofa listening to Bach and eating peanuts and thinking with vague anticipation about her trip to the States. She'd never been in a jumbo jet before and was looking forward to that part of it as much as anything.

Jane stuck her head around the door.

'I say, can I borrow the animal for the evening?'

'Sure. You know where it is, don't you?' The animal was a fur stole of indeterminate species which Henry had picked up at a jumble sale and given to Alex one Christmas. It looked surprisingly good on Jane, with her classic, rather staid style of dressing, while on Alex it always looked odd, like an afterthought. She had decided that she'd give it to Jane if and when they ended their flat share. But the flat share was starting to feel more and more like a permanent state of affairs, at least as far as their immediately foreseeable futures were concerned. This was a depressing thought to both of them, as the arrangement was never meant to be more than a stop-gap, a brief interlude en route to better things. Better things were proving elusive.

'There, how do you like it?' Jane was wearing a simple low-cut black dress, her newly washed hair hanging loose, and had a silver handbag clutched in her hand and the animal thrown casually over one shoulder.

'You look wonderful,' sighed Alex, and added quite sincerely, though it came out sounding slightly sour, 'Very classy. You'll kill 'em dead.'

'We're having drinks first at David's, I'm only about half an hour late, but if he phones tell him I've just left.'

'And if Martin phones you're still in Bath.'

'Yes, well, just say you haven't seen me for yonks. That's far better in case I have to cook up some sort of excuse. Anyway, have a lovely evening and give a big kiss to Digger for me. Byeee.'

'Bye bye,' and she added dutifully, trying not to sound as patronising as Jane did, 'Have a nice time.'

Saying goodbye to Jane was the one operation which had not yet benefited from the spontaneity which was gradually permeating their relationship. Was it Jane's last-minute instructions, which were always given in a bossy, impersonal way, Alex wondered, or could it be, this time, that she was slightly jealous of Jane? Jealous of what? Her glossy blonde good looks, so coveted by boring status-seeking older men like David and Martin? Or her ability to sparkle in the predictable routines demanded of her at Sara's up-market parties? Or the invitations themselves?

Alex tried to remember how long it was since she'd been invited to a proper party where everyone dressed up and there was champagne and canapés and a hostess who circulated and introduced people? Or even, come to think of it, a proper dinner party with twelve carefully selected guests and witty conversation and five courses of good food and long anecdotes over the port? Even six guests and three courses seemed to be a thing she hadn't come across since her time with Hugh, and a series of evenings with people they had characterized as victims of early middle age: an intelligent wife, housebound with young children, entertaining her husband's unappreciative colleagues and their unpredictable girlfriends and second wives, who would most likely never reciprocate.

She usually accepted that it was a good thing that she was out of that kind of social scene because she considered herself temperamentally ill-equipped to cope with it: too reserved in formal situations, and unable to project an interesting façade except in one-to-one conversation.

It was, in some permutation or other, the world of most of her acquaintances, and she was well aware that rather than having manoeuvred herself out of it, as she imagined she had, there was the possibility that she'd simply been dropped, because she didn't fit in easily. But that didn't bother her – she had once remarked that she was the last person she'd want to invite if she gave a dinner party herself.

But, as she lay on the sofa putting peanuts in her mouth one by one, she began to remember an evening about eight or nine years previously when she was staying at Digger's father's place during the summer term of her first year at university. The old man, as they called him, had decided to give a dinner party with his mistress, Shirley, a vivacious South African widow of Jewish origin, as hostess. Two local girls were employed to help the cook-housekeeper, the assembled company had all previously passed some kind of Shirley test so that they never questioned the set-up. Alex remembered with especial fondness the way that Shirley had announced at coffee time that the ladies had no intention of retiring, but would assume the status of honorary gentlemen and remain at table during the port on the understanding that this would not be allowed to inhibit the conversation, and then tried to put everyone at their ease by telling an off-colour story. That, and the memory of the crême brulée, and a disconcerting remark by the old man towards the end of the evening indicating to Alex that he rather fancied her, threatened to overwhelm her with nostalgia.

Spaghetti Bolognese with Digger seemed a dull prospect for the evening ahead. It was already half past eight and Alex began to get impatient at his lateness. She was perched on the edge of the Chesterfield looking at an empty wine glass and an empty peanut bowl and wondering what music to play when the doorbell rang. Digger. And she was in the wrong mood.

'Hallo there. Long time no see.'

'Digger!' (heavily sarcastic) 'Here already?'

'God, am I late or something? I thought we just said after work. . . .'

'Probably. I knocked off at five. Come in anyway. I'm in a foul mood in case you hadn't noticed.'

'Well, never mind, here's a six-pack, cheer you up. . . .'

'Oh, Digger, you are the limit.' It was an expression she hadn't heard for years, and then one she was more accustomed to receiving than giving. 'You know I never drink canned beer.' It sounded peevish with overtones of Jane. 'Oh, sod it, I'm sorry. Let's go to the pub and have a drink and I'll pick up some plonk on the way.'

'God, you *are* in a funny mood,' muttered Digger, as Alex pushed him out of the front door again with a grim smile on her face.

They sat on the floor leaning their backs on the Chesterfield, empty spaghetti plates piled on a tray by the door, and listened to a new LP that Digger had brought with him. It was one of those ambitious mixtures of pop musicians and classical orchestra and choir that had never appealed to Alex. One particularly strident and pretentious passage sent her into a fit of laughter. Digger was almost offended.

'Come on, it's not that awful,' he said with reproachful good humour.

'No, wait, wait,' Alex recovered herself and leaned over to turn the volume down. 'It's just what it reminded me of . . . you remember that evening when Shirley and the old man gave a dinner party, it's an exact parallel, everything *apparently* so classic and correct and awfully English, except for Shirley, and then the terrible blue stories over the port with all the ladies looking frightfully brave, and Shirley suddenly telling everyone that I'd probably had it more times than I'd had hot dinners − the same sort of combination that either works wonderfully or just jars . . . do you know what I mean?'

'Yes, sort of,' said Digger. 'Do you know, I'd forgotten all about that evening. It seems like another world, doesn't it?'

'Mmmm. Rather superb in its way.'

'But you don't like the record?'

'No, I think it's crap.' Alex laughed at her apparent incon-sistency. 'What I mean is it's the same sort of tightrope, once you leave the conventions behind. Either it works well and its incredibly enjoyable, or else its ghastly, cringe-making, you know. . . . She cringed and gestured towards the speakers, then went on, 'It's funny, I was thinking about that dinner party earlier on. I never seem to get invited to that sort of thing nowadays.'

'Well, it was pretty damn unique,' said Digger, chuckling at the memory. 'I go to some political ones, quite good back-ground really, but I don't think I'd bother unless it was good for me career-wise.'

'Good Lord, you do take it all seriously, don't you?' Alex meant to imply simple curiosity, but Digger felt provoked to defensiveness.

'Oh, for Christ sake, what the hell is wrong with that? Yes, of course I take it seriously. I want to get somewhere, have some real power before I'm too old, be someone who counts instead of sitting back and watching mediocre careerists climb-ing up the ladder. It's the only way that what I believe in can be any use to anyone else.'

'Who?'

'Well, my constituents presumably, for a start. Once I have a constituency that is.' He knew he was sounding pompous, so he attacked: 'I can't understand this dilettante attitude of yours. You're obviously damn good at what you do, and you could have been a brilliant academic, but you just don't seem to put yourself into anything with any commitment. You don't have any structure, any ambitions.'

They'd had this argument before, it didn't bother Alex much. She brought out her usual reply.

'But it leaves me very free, doesn't it? As long as I can pay the bills from week to week I can jump in any direction I want. I'm not stuck with some middle class preconception of a "useful career" or whatever.'

'But you don't jump.'

'Oh, I think about it. Maybe I'm just lazy. I was thinking of teaching next year, getting an adult education course together on contemporary fiction and dropping the guidebook stuff.'

'That's not exactly stretching yourself, is it?'

'Well, there you go again. The middle class morality! Why should I stretch myself before I'm ready? I've got lots of long-term ideas, I'd like to write a really good literary biography for example, but I don't want to commit myself to the wrong topic just for the sake of doing a book. There's plenty of time for everything.'

'There! That's exactly what you lack. You've got no sense of urgency at all. The world as we know it might come to an end next week and you wouldn't even notice.'

'Oh, Jane would probably keep me informed via the *Daily Express*.' She meant it as a joke, Digger often criticised Jane's political naïvety.

'That bloody woman! She's becoming the most pernicious influence on you. It's all very well for her to ponce around being totally frivolous, but you're far too bright for that sort of thing. You start off by pretending to copy some of her mindless upper class affectations because it's funny, and end up by finding that's all that's left of you, a sparkling façade and no substance.'

'Oh, come on, that's not fair to me or Jane.'

'Well then, what *is* important to you, what really matters, what do you care about?'

The music had stopped. A car passed the window, its tyres swishing through the rain. Alex moved on her knees over to the pile of records and sat back on her heels. Digger went on taunting her.

'Don't be evasive, come on, what the hell do you really care about? What do you believe in?'

'Well, that's easy enough. You know I'm a Catholic.'

'Oh, come off it, Alex, someone as bright as you can't really believe in all that rubbish.'

They'd been through this argument before too, and Alex was not going to try and explain again about faith being faith and the clergy and the rules a thing apart that she refused to allow to cut her off from the essential core. Digger was obviously determined not to understand.

'Sometimes I get so annoyed with you, Digger. If it's not a point of view fully endorsed by the features pages of the *Guardian*, you seem incapable of understanding it. Your mind won't go beyond a certain narrow English intellectualism. . . .'

'Oh, my God, English. Next you're going to tell me that the reason that I can't understand you is because you're *Irish*. . . .'

She was angry now. 'Of course I'm fucking Irish! What the hell do I have to do, show you my bloody passport? Jesus Christ, Digger.'

'Catholics shouldn't swear like that. I always believed it was a sin.'

He was pathetic. Not even worth getting angry with. She ignored him and reached for her current favourite record instead – a Palestrina mass. Digger was so insensitive that with any luck he probably wouldn't even realise it was sacred music.

Digger slid off the Chesterfield where he'd retreated during their discussion and down to Alex's level.

'Sorry, love,' he said. 'I didn't mean to upset you, it was very facetious of me. I'm a bit on edge tonight. Kiss and make up?'

She shied away. Beautiful strains of Palestrina, intertwined voices, filled the room, calming her. She always thought of it as balm for the soul, a cool white scented balm running over her aching forehead, smoothing out the knots inside.

'Isn't it magic?' she said to Digger, relaxing again. 'Imagine, there's people who've never listened to Palestrina. Isn't that awful?'

Digger couldn't resist it. 'That's exactly what I mean,' he said quietly, 'when I talk about wanting to do something. I know I must seem very obvious and ordinary about it, but most people are, you know. You're very special.'

'No sense. That's what Tomás always tells me – "you'll never get sense". I don't know that I want to!' They both laughed a little.

'I hate to think what's going to become of you, damn you,' said Digger.

'Nothing much, I suppose.' She didn't know why she said it. Digger was being far nicer than usual. He must be softening her up for something. Here it comes, she thought.

'There's something I meant to tell you earlier, but you were in such an awful mood.'

'What?'

'I don't quite know how to put it.'

'You're engaged to be married,' she said in her Jane voice. It was a Jane-like thing to say.

Digger said incredulously, 'How did you know?'

'I didn't. I just guessed. It's not so difficult.'

'You're extraordinary, quite extraordinary.'

She ignored the flattery, which was becoming a bit cloying. 'Come on, tell me all about it, who is she?'

'Well, that's the thing, you see. She's very young, only twenty, but she's so wonderful that I can't let her get away. The only thing is that she's terribly jealous. She'll get over it eventually, but the trouble is I told her all about you, and she couldn't take it, made the most awful scene, and she wants me to stop seeing you. In fact she won't talk to me again until I've told you that.'

'Oh.'

'I'm sorry, Alex, it isn't the way I thought it would turn out. . . .'

'I never thought about it at all. We both knew it wouldn't go on forever, and at least it's a nice ending for one of us. Anyway, I'm still seeing Andy, don't forget.'

'Of course, I must tell Elizabeth that, she'll be very impressed. I just wish she could be a bit more civilised about things. She's got absolutely obsessed about you. I think she feels threatened because you've known me for so long. She doesn't even want to meet you, but I've told her that's ridiculous, you've got to come to the wedding.'

'Oh, don't worry, Digger, she'll get used to the idea.'

'Well, I don't like it much.' He paused. 'Maybe you and I will meet up in another ten years' time and have another affair.'

'Honestly, Digger, that's a terrible way to talk! Anyway, I bet you're divorced long before then.'

He looked shocked, and she regretted it. 'I'm sorry, Digger, I didn't mean it. We're always rubbing each other up the wrong way, it wouldn't have lasted much longer anyway, would it?'

Even before his engagement announcement she'd decided she didn't want to sleep with him any more. The novelty had worn off. It was, she thought, as Digger picked up their plates and went to do the washing-up before leaving, a dreary end to a dreary evening.

She put the Palestrina on again to cheer herself up.

*　　*　　*

Andy went off on his UK tour and Alex found that she missed having Digger around. So when Hugh phoned up, apparently quite sober, and asked if she fancied meeting for a drink, she accepted, even though she had not seen him since the night that Tom had been in London.

She had been spending so much time recently either working or with Andy that she was out of touch with most other people. Yet when she got to the point of sitting down at the telephone, address book in hand, to organise some 'social life' as she called it nowadays, she always found that there was no one in particular that she wanted to spend time with anyway.

She was quite happy staying in alone working through the new novels that piled up beside her desk and listening to Gregorian chants and Palestrina. She'd stopped drinking wine when she stayed in alone, because if she tried to read at the same time she found that she fell asleep, so she drank jasmine tea and felt very virtuous and calm. As long as she was busy reading, or thinking and writing about what she'd read, she was all right. She didn't take walks so often now, as she found they provoked too much introspection. Thinking about herself reactivated the unease that she had been experiencing lately, the unease that came from her feeling of being in a state of transition without knowing from what to where or what. The closest she could get to defining it was that this can't be all there is to life, there must be something better, but what? There was nothing in her life that she wanted to change, but somehow what she had was not enough, it left a void. Until she could define the unease better, she couldn't attack it, so she avoided thought, believing that time would do the trick.

She did not want to see Hugh in the flat again, just to be on the safe side, so she lied to him and said she'd be up in Fleet Street until late, so why didn't they meet in the wine bar behind Sloane Square. It would save her the long walk from the tube to her flat.

It was crowded when she got there, but she spotted Hugh immediately sitting at a tiny round table in front of a bottle of Perrier water, reading the evening paper. He stood up as she approached.

'Alex my love! Wonderful to see you. Take a seat, what can I get you?'

She tried not to look too surprised. He was obviously on his very best behaviour.

'Are you on Perryuch? Whatever next, don't tell me you've signed the pledge!' She kissed him on the cheek. 'Hugh, you've lost weight! You look wonderful.'

'Signed the what, you silly old tart!' That had always been his favourite term of endearment for Alex, as it was for all the women in his life. 'I'm on a diet, giving the old system a chance to recover. Red or white?'

'Red, I think. Look, don't worry, I'll get it. . . .'

But he was already on his way to the bar. She glanced at his paper and saw a review of Andy's latest LP. It was a good one, and she didn't notice Hugh coming back until he broke her concentration by asking, 'What's that? Have you got a piece in tonight?'

'No, but they're reviewing Andy's record. Good review. Remember Andy? You met him at the flat once?'

'Yeah, that bloody half-assed little pop star . . . I see your stuff in there quite often. You're keeping busy?'

'Oh yes, everything's fantastic. Cheers!'

They exchanged news with curiosity and satisfaction on both sides. Hugh was now involved with a BBC researcher who was away for a few days on an assignment. It seemed he'd had some sort of crisis over Christmas which had led to his decision to cut out drinking for a few weeks and lose some weight. Then he had moved from the tabloid to a more demanding but highly paid job with an American news agency, and decided to stay off the booze while he settled in. His new woman had two children from a previous marriage, and if, as he said with some distaste, he could get used to the idea of living with another man's offspring, he would probably marry her.

Compared with that, Alex felt that she didn't really have much to offer in the way of news. Under Hugh's persistent questioning she admitted that she was not (as he feared) screwing every bloke she met. She then rather over-emphasised the pleasures of her affair with Andy and her excitement at the forthcoming trip to the States with him. She had, she hoped, given Hugh the impression that she was a lot more stable and in control of her life than she actually felt.

She'd forgotten what good company Hugh could be when

sober, and the evening was very enjoyable. They went on to a new American-style restaurant where Hugh devoured an immense Waldorf salad and another bottle of Perrier while he watched Alex get through a massive plate of spare ribs and a small carafe of red wine.

She ordered a coffee, and Hugh lit up a cigar. It suited him, and she looked at him with a warm fondness that she had not anticipated.

'It's really nice to see you again, you know,' she said. 'It's silly how people get out of touch, I don't like it.'

'Well, you pissed off to the auld sod with your offshore bog-trotter, didn't you? I phoned you just before Christmas and Jane said you were in Castletown whatsit with Tomarse and you wouldn't be back in town for absolutely yonks.' He imitated Jane's voice with cruel accuracy.

'Christ, she would!'

'Why shouldn't she?'

'Well . . .' It seemed years ago, not a mere three months.

'I thought we'd lost you for good. She said it was all *on* again.'

'It was.' She knocked back half her coffee. 'Then we screwed it up again. I came back early.' Her voice sounded thin and lost in her own ears, and very unhappy.

'A fine man that Tom character, first-class fellow. He's worth a hundred Andy O'Sullivans.'

'Andy's nothing special to me. He's just an old friend I'm hanging around with at the moment.' But she was secretly pleased that Hugh thought she and Andy were more seriously involved. It saved her from having to admit to him that there was no one special in her life at the moment.

'But he's getting his leg over, isn't he?'

'Oh, for Christ sake, Hugh. Is that all that matters?'

He shook his head. 'Alex Buckley, you are not the sort of girl you're pretending to be. That's not your scene and you know it. He'll use you while it suits him, then he'll drop you. You need a real man like that Tom character, that's what you need.'

It was mostly anger at Hugh's assumption that he knew what was good for her that started her tears. It was the way that he spoke as if he had some kind of superior knowledge of life that came from knowing that there was a neat pattern which everyone's life somehow fitted into. That started her crying, then it was fear, fear that maybe he was right and life did indeed consist of some kind of predetermined grid, and everyone sooner or later found a niche in the grid which fitted them, and settled into it, everyone that is except *her*. She was condemned to wander forever alone, searching for something that would make sense of it all, searching for the secret which enabled other people to come to terms with it all.

'Alex my love, I didn't mean to upset you,' Hugh was all concern, and gently offered her a red silk handkerchief. 'I never realized Andy meant so much to you, come on. . . .'

'Oh, Christ, it's not that.' She mopped at the tears. If there was one thing she was not crying about it was Andy. Nor was it Digger's and Hugh's matrimonial plans. But still hot tears rolled down her face. 'And it's not Tom either,' she added in a defensive voice. 'Tom's impossible. Do you know what he's done?'

She hadn't told anyone this yet, not even Jane, and smiled through her tears, narrowing her eyes as a prelude to the revelation. 'He's bought a pub and a massive house with it and he wants me to go over and help him run it, start a restaurant and manage the staff and do bloody pub grub. . . .'

She broke off giggling because she thought Hugh would laugh at that. The idea of herself behind a counter in a white apron popping cheese sandwiches into the microwave oven and pulling pints of Guinness. . . .

But he didn't laugh, he took it quite seriously.

'And what's wrong with that? Eh?' A pause while he put on an expression which Alex used to call his uncle Hugh face. 'Alex my dear, you may think you're destined for greater things, but personally I can think of nothing nicer than having my own establishment in a nice quiet seaside town with the love of my life for company. . . .'

'Oh, Hugh! Castletown Berehaven is *not* a nice seaside town, it's the end of the bloody world, it doesn't even get tourists. And Tom's just antediluvian, male chauvinist pig doesn't come into it, he's got no idea. Anyway, I'd go mad if I had to work in a pub, whoever I was living with. Jesus Christ, all day everyday standing there in the dark pulling bloody pints and listening to the same old jokes hour after hour. . . .'

She stopped abruptly and hated herself. It wasn't true. She loved Castletown Berehaven precisely because it wasn't a nice seaside town in a touristic way and Tom's attitude to women was not something she could abstract from his whole being and point to as an excuse for not wanting to live with him. And she knew that it was not part of Tom's plan to leave her standing in a bar all day pulling pints. He probably wouldn't let her near his precious Guinness. But she could think of no other way to express her distaste for the idea of living with Tom to Hugh, and her distaste at least did register with him.

'So you've gone off Castletown Berehaven now, have you? I thought you were planning to go back there to live one of these days.' He leant back and puffed on his cigar, looking smug. 'So the big smoke's got its claws into you at last, eh? Fame and fortune have struck. You've finally grown up, you're one of us now, kiddo, you'll never go back now.'

Hugh looked comfortably pleased with himself. She shook her head, not crying any more in spite of the taunt in his last remark. She didn't even bother to get annoyed at being called 'kiddo'. Hugh was just one more person who didn't understand and it didn't matter much what he said. He had no solutions, he knew no answers, it was pointless to try to explain anything to him, and anyway how could she when she didn't even know what she wanted to explain.

'Forget it, I'm sorry, Hugh. It's been a bit of a long day. I must be somewhat – a hmmm – "overtired and emotional".'

She wasn't really, but it was one of Hugh's favourite expressions, and she knew that anyone who admitted to being in that state had an immediate claim on his sympathy.

He paid the bill and gave her a lift to her flat, and waited in his car, the smug smile still on his face, while she let herself in the front door. As she turned around to wave goodbye he rolled the window down and shouted, 'Welcome to the club, kiddo! You're one of us now.'

'How fucking wrong you are,' she muttered to herself as she closed the front door behind her. And she smiled and felt more light-hearted than she had done for months. She had not sorted it out, but she had not given up either. As long as she hadn't given up, anything could happen, and when it did she wasn't going to fight it. She'd be ready for it.

DISINTEGRATION

From Bantry to Bearhaven by land there is nothing remarkable, except the iron furnaces at Comolin, which have been in a thriving condition for some years past; but wood begins to grow very scarce. In the bay of Glengarriff, and towards the north-west part of Bantry Bay, they dredge up large quantities of coral sand, found to be a most excellent manure, and lasts in the ground above twenty years. At Ross Mac Owen, midway between Bearhaven and Bantry, lives Mr Murtough O'Sullivan, a person well known in those parts. He and his elder brother, who is commonly called Mac Fineen Duff, who lives near the river of Kinmair, are the chief remains of the O'Sullivan family in this country. There is in Spain a descendant of O'Sullivan Bear, who is ennobled, and called there Count of Bearhaven, and is also said to be hereditary governor of the Groyne.

Smith's Ancient and Present
State of the County and City of Cork
Dublin 1750, ed. Robert Day, Cork 1893

In the latter part of July the weather brightened considerably and it only rained on about one day in three. There were more tourists about – Dutch and German and French campers and hikers – and a different crop of yachts tied up daily alongside the local trawlers. Alex's life had evolved a new pattern.

She was reading again, reading with a curiosity and absorption that she hadn't known since she first discovered her liking for books in childhood. But she could never have predicted that the books she now read so eagerly would be old history books. She'd never had much time for history books before.

There was a stack of them in a glass-fronted book case which stood in a dark corner of the hallway near the unused front door. She'd always assumed these were law books, because the few titles you could make out easily without opening the cabinet were legal ones. But the great majority of the rest were nineteenth-century books on Irish history and accounts of travels through Ireland in the 1700s and 1800s.

The most interesting were the ones most closely concerned with the history of Cork and Kerry, and best of all were the ones about the Beara and the two great O'Sullivan septs – the O'Sullivan Bear of the Beara and the O'Sullivan Mór of neighbouring Kerry. Of all the O'Sullivans, one man stood out for Alex: Morty Óg O'Sullivan Beare. One branch of the O'Sullivan Bear lived as exiled noblemen in Spain. Donal O'Sullivan of Dunboy, Prince of Beare and Bantry, left Ireland for Coruña in the early 1600s at the same time as the Northern Chieftains O'Neill and O'Donnell, after heroic attempts to resist the far better equipped forces of Elizabeth 1. But it was Morty Óg, younger son in a family of descendants of the heroic Donal, who interested Alex. Morty was a distinguished officer of the Wild Geese fighting for the Catholic cause in the European wars of the mid-eighteenth century.

After Culloden he returned to Berehaven sailing a fast privateer under letters of marque from the French, which he used in smuggling operations to humiliate the English and also to bring some much-needed wealth to the pockets of his dispossessed kin. Morty Óg – to the English a formidable enemy described as smuggler, pirate and outlaw, to the inhabitants of Europe a respected nobleman and warrior, and to the people of the Beara a hero whose popularity was legendary even in his own lifetime – managed to bring the past alive for Alex.

Alex now slept with piles of books on and beside her bed and often fell asleep reading, to be woken in the night by a hefty nineteenth-century analysis of the shortcomings of eighteenth-century policy on corn and wool taxation digging in her ribs.

In the mornings she stayed in bed reading, making one trip to the kitchen to feed the cat and boil a kettle for a cup of coffee. She got up mid-afternoon, pulled on her jeans, an old red check shirt, her tatty baneen sweater and sea boots, breakfasted on soda bread and a boiled egg or a rasher as quickly as she could, then, taking her yellow oilskin from its hook by the kitchen door, went off for her daily walk.

It seemed that early evening was the least likely time of day for rain. It was light until after ten, and there were often spectacular sunsets which she liked to watch from the Bere-haven Inn on her return.

Her walk always followed the same route. She was out of the town within five minutes and soon turned off the main coast road on to a smaller track which was so seldom used that grasses and weeds had taken root among the shiny tarmac gravel in the middle of it. A bewildering profusion of wild flowers sprouted among the cow parsley and wild garlic in the tall hedges. The only sound, besides her own footsteps, was the wind whistling around the wires on the telegraph poles. She carried a switch in her hand, and used it from time to time to swipe the heads from some dandelions or to tap against her sea boots rythmically as she walked.

The road climbed over a headland and on certain curves she could glimpse the sea and distant cliffs. It took a good hour before she reached the sign saying 'Private Ard na Gashel Farm'. Here she turned off the road and picked her way across a strong-smelling cattle grid on to the dirt track that ran down to the farm yard. Coming out of the yard she followed a sheltered grassy lane, unused for years, that led to a ruined stone built cottage. It was nearly smothered in green vegetation, and the corrugated iron roof had turned a rich rust colour and split.

Beyond the tighín the grassy path was even smaller and overgrown with ferns and brambles. It twisted around the hillside climbing over a small bluff to the hidden sea inlet. There was a narrow stony beach there at low tide, and a fresh water spring where she stopped to drink and splash her face with cool water. But her destination was the headland which formed the west shelter for the tiny bay. She climbed up to it along a path of springy turf that ran above the rocks, and at the very end she collapsed into a natural armchair formed by thick grass growing over a rocky hollow.

In the hollow she had shelter from the wind whatever direction it was coming from and the slightest suspicion of sunshine made it warm enough to take off her sweater, and sometimes her shirt and trousers too. She passed hours there, not thinking, but looking and listening.

She could hear the delicate clear song of the land birds in the distance, but this was often obliterated by the piercing calls of the gulls and harsh croaks and caws from the rarer sea birds who nested on the opposite headland. At first she had found it un-nerving to have these big hawk-like creatures circling above her as soon as she'd sat down. The creaking of their wings made her turn, suspecting rabbits in the grass, then a shadow fell across her and she looked up to see a pre-historic creature wheeling away back to the nest, screaming angrily at the invasion. But she discovered that after the one tour of inspection they didn't bother her again.

She could spend hours just watching a few blades of coarse grass ruffling in the sea breeze, standing out in silhouette against the calm green water of the inlet below. Higher up she could see the rocks of the opposite headland and watch the sea climbing up the black seaweed at their base until it reached the edge of the granite. Some days it broke against the rocks in satisfying gushes of white foam. Above the water line there were bright yellow lichen patches on the dark rock, and then a field of dark green gorse.

Sometimes she could hear a tractor in the very remote distance, churning up and down some cliffside field. For about a week there was the constant monotonous drone of a chain-saw up on some neighbouring farm. And every day at six o'clock the lowing of the cows as they were brought in for milking was carried down to her.

She liked it best of all when boats passed on their way up to Castletownbere or Bantry. The trawlers were always too far out for her to hear more than the muffled throb of their engines, but at this time of year there were quite a few yachts passing in close. She guessed that if they were on this side of the inlet they must have come up through the Dursey Sound from Kenmare Bay. When she talked to the crews later in Castletownbere she discovered that most of them had in fact come around the Mizen Head from Crookhaven or Schull.

She would first be alerted by a creaking halyard, a flapping sail. Then she could watch them from her hollow without being seen and could hear quite clearly the conversations on board. Today it was: 'Pass up another bottle of Murphy's, willya, Mick? . . . Jesus Mary and Joseph, what kind of shagging bird is that?'

A Kinsale boat? She checked the stern, KYC. Maybe Mick Roche was the man below decks. She'd find out later in Shanahan's.

Sometimes the voices were English, and once she eavesdropped on a French yacht whose crew were arguing pedantically about whether the place that they were heading for was called Castletownbere, Castletown Bearhaven, or simply Berehaven.

So the hours passed in a series of small moments. Sometimes she dozed, adding to her already formidable log of hours slept.

It was soon the case that her day was not complete without a visit to Ard na Gashel. There was an important added attraction since she had discovered a newly concreted landing stage with an iron mooring ring laid into the rocks immediately below the place where she lay. It had been built in such a way that it was completely invisible from both sea and land. She hadn't told anyone about it, not even Tom. She reckoned that certain local fishermen had an understanding with the farm and were using it out of season to land their illegal salmon catch, or something similar. The salmon explanation was probably true, and she liked it the more because she saw the poaching as a continuation of the traditions of her new hero Morty Óg.

She had become quite unreasonably fond of Morty Og and one day was taken aback to find that she could, with no particular effort, vividly imagine him standing on the green turf above the grey rocks of the landing stage in the uniform

93

(now rather the worse for wear) of a French officer – a brown leather cross-belt, a dark plumed hat in his hand, long black hair flowing in the stiff breeze, his body tensed, lean and strong and tall (she had got furious with one historian she'd come across who, obviously ignorant of the significance of Morty's surname, had described him as stocky and bear-like), gazing out to sea, searching the horizon for the arrival of the brig from La Rochelle which would unload casks of claret and brandy for Morty Óg to distribute among the decadent gentry and then load up with equally contraband sheep fleeces for the French supplied by his kinsmen. She reckoned she knew exactly what was going on.

So strong was her fantasy of Morty Óg that she began to feel uneasy out at Ard na Gashel point, as if she were no longer alone when she stretched out in her nest of grass above the landing stage.

So strong was her sense of Morty's presence there day after day in rain or mist or sunshine, but especially in sunshine, that, on one particularly bright day when Morty seemed less preoccupied than usual with the horizon, she caught herself opening her mouth to shout goodbye at him as she got up to leave. He was quite definitely there, but this time he was wearing jeans and a dark blue sweater. Her sudden appearance as she rose up from the hidden grassy hollow where she'd been lying seemed to have startled him as much as his transformation into modern dress startled her. And it got worse: he smiled at her and shouted, 'Ola.'

She had no idea what it was all about, but Morty's wide smile meant only one thing to her: he didn't object to her presence there, he knew she was in the right place, he knew she belonged. And he didn't mind her being able to see him.

The only thing that it occurred to her to say as she waved goodbye was, 'Go raibh maith agat, Morty Óg.'

His answer echoed in her mind all the way back to Castletown Berehaven:

'Ta fáilte romhat, aléanabh.'

*   *   *

'Tomás.'

'Alex.'

She pulled a bar stool up to her usual corner between the door and the window and rested her sea boots on a ledge of the bar.

'And what'll it be today?'

'A glass of Murphy's when you've a minute there.'

'Very funny.'

The only other person in the bar was old Seany Harrington sitting on the settle beside the fire staring into his pint.

'Grand day,' said Tomás gently as he put her glass on the counter and picked up some change from the pile of silver she'd left there.

'Will you have one yourself?'

'No thanks, I'm okay there.'

He nodded towards a glass of whiskey which he kept constantly topped up from the optic. She always offered, he always refused.

'Tomás. . . .'

'What can I do for you?'

'What does it mean when someone says something to you like, uh . . . "Ta fáilte romhat, aléanabh"?'

'Jeez, aren't you learning fast now. Who was it taught you that one? The múinteoir?' The local schoolteacher, known as the múinteoir because of his enthusiasm for the Irish, drank in Shanahan's.

'No, no, I just heard it now out at Ard na Gashel.'

'And why would anyone be saying that to you?'

'Well, that's what I want to know.' She should have waited and asked the múinteoir later on. This was turning into one of Tom's blackguarding sessions.

'You're forever going out to Ard na Gashel. I don't know what you see in it at all.'

'It's nice there.' She had to get him back to the Irish. 'Agus tá an aimsir go brea. Tá se go-hiontach amuigh.' (And it's lovely weather. It's wonderful outside.)

'Is maith sin! Tá tu ag foighlam go tapaidh.' (That's great. You're learning quickly.)

'Go raibh maith agat.' (Thank you.)

'Ta fáilte romhat, aléanabh.'

'There, you said it! Come on, what does it mean?'

' "Ta fáilte romhat" is an old-fashioned courtesy, something like "not at all, you're welcome", that kind of thing. And aléanabh" is a term of endearment, it means child, but something like darling as well.'

'Go raibh maith agat. Agus sláinte!'

'Ta fáilte romhat, aléanabh. Agus sláinte.'

On the left, as we enter the harbour, is Beare Island, and on the opposite and western shore the village of Castletown Bearehaven, to the south of which are the ruins of the famous Castle of Dunboy, once the stronghold of O'Sullivan Beare, now in the possession of Mr Puxley.

Mr Puxley, of Dunboy, was shot by Morty Oge O'Sullivan in 1754. A military party was dispatched from Cork to Bearehaven to apprehend the murderer. O'Sullivan had fortified his house, which he defended till his ammunition was exhausted, when he rushed forth and broke through his enemies, but when clearing a hedge, was shot through the heart.

O'Sullivan's body was lashed to the stern of a king's cutter, and towed through the sea, to Cork, where his head was spiked on the South-gate. Some of O'Sullivan's followers were killed and others wounded in his defence.

History of Cork, Vol. II, Rev. C. B. Gibson, 1861

The sun on Ivera no longer shines brightly;
The voice of her music no longer is sprightly;
No more to her maidens the light dance is dear,
Since the death of our darling O'Sullivan Beare.

Had he died calmly I would not deplore him;
Or if the wild strife of the sea war closed o'er him;
But with ropes round his white limbs through ocean to rail him,
Like a fish after slaughter, tis therefore I wail him.

Dear head of my darling, how gory and pale
These aged eyes see thee high spiked on their jail;
That cheek in the summer sun ne'er shall grow warm,
Nor that eye e'er catch light but the light of the storm.

A curse, blessed ocean, is on thy green water,
From the harbour of Cork to Ivera of slaughter,
Since thy billows were dyed with the red wounds of fear,
Of Muiertach Oge, our O'Sullivan Beare.

Verses from *The Lament of Muiertach Oge's Nurse*

Translated from the Irish by
J. J. Callanan

Alex and Conor were in the bedroom of Andy's suite smoking a joint. Outside a party was slowly getting under way. Record company people and management people were drifting in and out pouring themselves drinks from a well-stocked trolley. Andy and the group had not yet arrived back from the gig. It had, everyone agreed, been a great success. The local audience loved them. They were not due to play again until Saturday, in two days' time, when they would make the recording as planned. By Sunday Alex and Conor would be free to fly back to London.

So far the trip had gone remarkably smoothly. Andy had managed to avoid being alone with Alex, but had been kind and made sure that she had everything she needed. Conor had been as good to work with as she had anticipated, the hotel was not merely comfortable, but extraordinarily luxurious and she spent most of her spare time having long baths and showers and then lying on her bed watching the telly. She had been downtown with Conor a couple of times shopping and they'd both bought cowboy boots, jeans, check shirts, stetsons and Indian jewellery. The second time they were very high and had giggling fits in a drug store over their wide-eyed wonderment at the variety of products on sale. Conor said that must be how culchies felt on their first visit to Switzers in Dublin, and Switzers became their nickname for the hotel, because they felt the same provincial awe at its luxury.

Conor picked up the TV remote control and flicked it on. He stared in disbelief:

'Oh God, Benny Hill! How unreal!'

Alex passed him back the joint, laughing helplessly. It was quite normal for her to be speechless when stoned. She hadn't had any grass for a long time, let alone good grass like this stuff. Andy had given her a packet, a conspiratorial look on his face, shortly after arriving saying: 'Welcome to America.' She'd guessed its contents immediately.

'I've got a great idea,' said Conor. 'Let's pick up a bottle of wine out there and go back to my room to watch Benny Hill.'

'Ah. Why not,' said Alex slowly. She had not been looking forward to the party as she found it a big effort to respond adequately to the goodwill and enthusiasm of Andy's American contacts. Whereas the three days she had spent in Conor's company working, shopping, eating and sharing impressions meant that she now felt totally at ease with him. On the flight over he had shown her photos of Karen, a very beautiful girl, with her work, vast paintings that reminded Alex of Robert Natkin. Karen and Conor were in the process of buying a house. Alex understood why she'd been told, and was happy for Conor.

The party had grown in their absence and was temporarily occupying part of the corridor so it was easy enough for Alex and Conor to disappear unnoticed and lift a plate of seafood canapés as well as a bottle of Californian rosé.

They had been given connecting rooms on the floor above Andy's suite. Alex of course immediately wondered whether that happened by coincidence or by Andy's intervention, and then decided she was being ridiculous.

This was the first time she had seen Conor's room. It was identical to hers, but rigidly neat and tidy. His camera bag was on the table surrounded by cartons of film next to his black loose-leaf notebook. He'd obviously unpacked all his clothes and hung them in the closet. There was a Flann O'Brien paperback on his bedside table which Alex noted approvingly, and a small radio casette player. The bed had been turned down at one corner for the night and his order for early morning wake-up placed on the pillow. Alex had left her tidiness at home, and her room was scattered with papers, notes, postcards, shopping, clean and dirty clothes, free gifts, half-read paperbacks and newspapers.

She stood in the doorway gaping as Conor flashed the television on, then finally managed to say, 'Hey, it's so tidy! I've turned next door into an instant slum, you should have a look.'

'Don't they tidy it up for you?'

'Oh, they try.' She laughed and put the seafood on a spare chair.

'Do you know what I've got to do?' asked Conor looking pained.

She was intrigued. 'No. What?'

He laughed and said slowly, emphasising each word: 'Take off these fucking boots.'

She fell on to one of the beds laughing. 'Oh, don't talk about it. Mine are absolutely killing me. I'll never get used to them.' She paused and tried to pull herself together, standing up and brushing down her jeans for no reason at all.

'Look, there's one way to deal with this,' she told him. 'Sit on that hard chair there with the food. I mean get rid of the food and sit there.'

More laughter.

Conor looked at her with his eyebrows raised and moved the food on to the table, putting his loose-leaf file on the floor. Then he sat down on the chair.

'Good,' said Alex. 'Now, give us a leg, and hold on.' She turned her back on him, gripped the leg he'd offered by the heel and had the boot off in one deft movement.

'Next,' she said. 'And you're doing the same for me after, all right?'

His second boot was off as quickly and he slumped down the chair watching Alex stand the two boots up together against the wall. He smiled at her in admiration.

'Jesus, the Anglos know how to do things.'

For a moment she didn't understand what he was getting at, then she replied with surprise:

'What do you mean Anglos? I'm not Anglo, come off it.'

'Who else would know how to take boots off like that? It's your scene.' He laid the Dublin accent on thickly. 'The likes of us, we only sees it on the telly.'

'Oh, come on, that's how you get sea boots off and I sail with a character who always wears too thick socks.' Tomás. 'It's much worse on a small boat with rubber boots.'

'Oh, I see, you're the yachting crowd, are you, not the huntin' crowd.' He had assumed, unconvincingly, an upper class Irish accent. She replied in the same hoity tones.

'I don't yacht, I sail.'

'Oh yeah, and I suppose your idea of a small boat is somewhere around thirty foot.' He laughed with an admiration so frank that she couldn't resist playing along.

'Thirty, thirty-five-ish. The ideal is supposed to be one foot for every year of the owner's age, and the feller I usually sail with is thirty-six. Now, come on, it's my turn.'

Conor didn't have the knack, or her boots were much tighter than his. In any case, her socks came off too, and the freedom felt great. However, her jeans, which she'd been persuaded by Conor to buy a size smaller than usual, were pinching her waist and her crotch. She picked up her handbag to get the key to her room.

'Hang on, I'm just going next door to take off these jeans. They're far too bloody tight.' She took a dog-eared notebook and her wallet out of the bag and peered into it. 'Oh hell, I've forgotten my key again. I'm always doing that . . . I know, can I borrow one of your Switzer robes, you know, those towelling things in the bathroom?'

'Go ahead. And bring a couple of glasses.'

They picked at the sea food, and when Benny Hill was followed by a local late night chat show Conor played with the remote control, finally settling mid-way through a Liz Taylor movie with an exotic seaside location. It was hard to follow the plot. There was a shot of green-clad cliffs, a whitewashed villa perched on top, and below the deep blue sea with white foam at the edges breaking on to dark jagged rocks. It made Alex sigh.

'What?' asked Conor who'd been half-dozing.

'Oh, the sea. It's a shame we're not near the coast. We could go for a walk or a swim or something.'

'We must be hours away from the sea.'

'Awful feeling really. I think I'll go to West Cork for a few days when I get back.'

'All right for some.'

'Oh, come on, they must be paying you a fortune as well.'

'Yeah, but it'll all go on the house. I'll need every penny for that.'

'Ah, but then you'll have the house, won't you?'

'You could start saving.'

'Can't be bothered. It'd be so long before I could afford anything I liked, I can't get interested in the idea at all.'

'Well, I expect you can feel like that if your family's loaded. I mean, if you've always had it you get a kind of confidence about material things, and you end up not caring about whether you have them or not.'

Alex thought about this briefly. She'd never associated her own lack of acquisitiveness with her comfortable family background. Maybe there was some truth in it.

'Yes, maybe. But I mean, my parents aren't particularly loaded, I never thought of myself in that category. I'd never expect them to do anything big for me like helping me to buy a flat or a car. But they are *there*, I suppose, if there was some real crisis. I'd just never thought it made any difference to how I felt about things – I mean about money.'

'What do they do?'

'They're doctors. My mother just works part-time now, and they're both retiring in a few years. Back to Kinsale.'

'Now that's a very Anglo town. What sort of place do they have there?'

'Aha,' said Alex. 'The parental bungalow, I call it. They sold my granny's house and built this modern labour-saving home.' She laughed uneasily as she always did at her refusal to approve of their decision.

'I always thought you came from some really cliché Anglo family, crumbling mansion in its own park and a load of mad uncles and horse-faced aunts.'

'Oh, I know the type – from books, I mean. Do you know, I've never actually met anyone like that. I think they're all in Wicklow, or else they're still such a tight clique that none of our crowd ever gets a look in.'

'So you're not Anglo-Irish at all?'

'No. I get called a West Brit in Kinsale, but they'd call you anything there. I've lived in London since I was four, but I've always spent a lot of time in Cork too, holidays and visits to relations. My father's a Catholic Buckley, and my mother was a Sullivan. They must have sold the O somewhere along the line, but she says they've always been Catholics. Some of them still farm in Kerry, but both sides are mainly ordinary Cork middle class professional types. That's as far as I know, I've never been very interested in family history and stuff.'

'What do you mean, "sold the O"?'

'God, don't they teach you jackeens anything?' She gave him a friendly slap on the chest with the back of her hand. '"Sold the O for a bowl of soup," they say in Cork. A method of conversion in the famine, so you usually reckon a Sul is one of the other crowd and an O'Sul is one of us.'

'Oh,' said Conor, making a mental note of the information.

'What does your dad do then?' asked Alex.

'Civil Service. Clerical grade, lower middle class. Came to

Dublin from Ballina in the forties, married a Ballina girl and had me and eight others.'

'Nine of you!'

'Oh, and that's not all. I've scores of first cousins up in Kilburn. The real London Irish, little girls in green and white dresses and pipe bands and the annual piss-up in Willesden Park. I keep meaning to do some photos up there, its unbelievable. And I've a crowd of uncles in the Boston police . . . weird.'

'I've never been into that London Irish thing.' She dredged her memory and said, 'I went to an Irish pub in Islington once.'

Conor laughed. 'Islington! Once! Fine London Irish you are. Don't you have any cousins in Croydon or Carshalton? That's where Cork people go if they can. One step up from Fulham.'

'No, they're all in Cork. It's just me and the parents in London.'

'Weird,' said Conor, his mind still half planning photos of the Willesden festival.

Liz Taylor was throwing a magnificent fit of anger, and they turned back to the television, each leaning back on the plump pillows of their own double bed.

They must have dozed off. Someone was knocking on the door and the television was buzzing. Alex stumbled to her feet, then it struck her that she was in Conor's room in a towelling bathrobe.

'Pssst, Conor,' she leant over and gave him a gentle push. 'There's someone at the door. I don't want to shock Switzers. You'd better open it, and I'll get dressed.'

She shut the bathroom door, and then remembered that she'd hung her new jeans over the back of Conor's chair. 'Blast.' She listened at the door and heard the outer door close.

Conor knocked on the bathroom door and handed her the jeans. 'It's okay, it's only Andy.'

'Blast,' she thought again. It annoyed her that it would now be assumed that she and Conor were sexually involved when it was such a pleasant change that they were not. 'It shouldn't matter anyway, it won't make any difference to anything.'

Maybe it would turn into another private joke between her and Conor, their 'great night of passion' at Switzers.

'Hallo, Andy.' He was with a blonde girl, her full breasts visible through her white T-shirt, who looked about fourteen years old.

'This is Labelle.'

'Hi there, Alex, I've been just dying to meet you.'

'Hallo, Labelle.'

'Alex, we've all been looking for you everywhere,' said Andy. 'There's an urgent message for you to phone this number.'

He put his hand under her elbow as if he expected her to collapse and showed her a piece of hotel notepaper with a two-figure number on it preceded by the words 'Castletown-bere' and 'urgent', the latter underlined three times.

'How strange,' she said, taking the paper from him.

'Reception were worried that the girl who took the message didn't get the rest of the number.'

'No, that's right. It's Shanahan's in Castletownbere. But I can't understand why.' As she looked round the circle of concerned faces the full potential of the message began to hit her.

'Oh, my God,' she said. 'Someone must have died.' It was such an unfamiliar thing to have to say and sounded so casual that she almost laughed. 'But why Castletown Berehaven?' She was thinking aloud through a process which had already happened in her mind. She wanted time to get used to it. 'It must be my aunt Kate and my parents have gone over to arrange the funeral.'

'I'm so sorry if it's Kate,' said Andy. 'She was a lovely person.'

'Of course I'm only guessing. I could be quite wrong. Maybe it's just Tomás trying to find out if I can help him deliver a boat or something.' It sounded highly unlikely, especially when she looked back to the note in her hand and saw the word 'urgent' underlined three times. 'No, he'd hardly bother to track me down here. It must be Kate. I'd better get to a phone. What time is it anyway?'

'Nearly half-three,' said Conor. He and Andy exchanged glances and Andy looked at Labelle who seemed on the point of tears. Andy and Conor both spoke at the same time:

'I'll go with . . . Shall I stay. . . .'

'No, no,' said Alex calmly. 'I'll be okay, I'll just put my jeans on and go and get my key, then I'll put a call through from my room. I'll be all right, really. . . .'

'Tell you what,' said Conor. 'I'll leave my connecting door open and if you want me you can come in and I'll be here.'

'Thanks, but I'll be fine. And thanks, Andy. I'm sorry you had to organise a search party.'

The time difference was perfect and it was ten at night when Alex got through to Shanahan's. Her unspoken worry was that something had happened to her parents and Kate had been selected by the family to break the news, but she kept telling herself that this was very unlikely. She distracted herself from that by imagining a highly involved melodrama with Tom at the centre of it, holding the clientele of Shanahan's hostage and making all kinds of threats that would be carried out unless she would speak to him and calm him down. She found the soap opera scenarios that were presenting themselves to her ridiculous, and was afraid that they indicated some kind of essential mediocrity in the quality of her mind. She made herself concentrate on the idea that Kate had died or was very ill, but when the switchboard rang back with her connection she felt a moment of panic so strong that she almost blacked out.

'Hallo.' It came out as a hoarse whisper.

'Hallo, caller, I have a line to Ireland for you. One moment please.'

It was Dublin. They had to dial Castletownbere, the local switchboard was still a manual one, and they took well over five minutes to answer. Alex kept looking at the door to Conor's room and wondering whether to fetch him or whether it would be easier alone. Then the switchboard had to connect with Shanahan's. She was getting into what she always referred to as 'a state' only because there was the possibility of calling Conor, who might or might not make things easier. If she'd been quite alone she wouldn't have got into such a state, she decided, so she willed herself to ignore the possibility of Conor.

Finally Shanahan's answered. The line was filthy, crows on the telegraph wires again, she thought, and she couldn't help cheering up a fraction.

'Hallo, hallo, it's Alex Buckley speaking. I had a message to call. Alex Buckley.'

'Ah, Mrs O'Connell's niece. One moment now.'

'Shit.' Whoever it was went away without saying who they'd gone to fetch. Even if that person was in the bar itself, which was unlikely, it gave her time to get Conor. He was still dressed, he'd been standing by, planning to phone her when she rang off and invite himself over to check that she was okay.

She rushed back to the phone, leaving the connecting door open, and Conor sat at the foot of the bed.

'They've gone to fetch someone,' Alex explained. 'Hallo, hallo.'

'Alex dear. Are you all right?' It was her mother. She felt immensely relieved, almost happy, and then a surge of guilt for momentarily forgetting Kate.

'Yes, I'm fine. What's happened?'

Kate had died peacefully in her sleep earlier that week. She'd been found the same day by some neighbours who'd worried because she hadn't taken in the milk. The funeral was on Saturday and Alex's mother just thought she'd like to know so that she could say a prayer. She hoped Alex wasn't too upset, everyone understood why she couldn't be there, and she hoped she wouldn't let it spoil her trip. Her parents would be back in London on Wednesday, and Alex arranged to meet them for dinner.

'There,' she said as she put down the phone. 'That wasn't too bad. I mean, it's really sad, but she died peacefully in her sleep, it could have been so much worse, and she was nearly seventy. She was a lovely person, you know. I'll miss her being there.'

She didn't want to talk any more. She'd already said too much, and nothing at all. It must, she thought, seem callous to be so calm.

She and Conor both stood up and Conor put his arms around her and pulled her head on to his shoulder saying matter of factly, 'You're great, you know.' She leant her full weight against Conor's body. His arms were strong and protective around her. She felt unreal, light-headed yet calm after the earlier turmoil of speculation.

'Do you know,' she said to Conor, her head still on his shoulder, 'for a while there I thought it was my parents had died and they'd got Kate to break the news. That's why I'm more relieved than anything. It's strange. It's the first time someone I know well has died, and it doesn't feel like I thought it would.'

Conor said nothing. They stood embraced for a long time, until finally he reached down and took her hand and led her into his room.

'You're right. Next door is a slum,' he said, teasing. He picked up a roach from the ashtray, lit it and passed it to Alex. 'That way you'll sleep like. . . .' He caught himself in time, and finished '. . . like a rock.'

She smiled at him, saying, 'I don't think we have to take this too seriously.'

'How do you mean?'

Oh gawd, she thought. What have I said? And answered, 'My aunt dying, I mean. It's just something sad for me, but I'll get used to it.'

He put his arm round her and kissed her very gently on the cheek several times. Their skin felt good together. 'You're great, you know.' He kissed her again and then repeated: 'You're great. And I don't think you should be alone tonight. But I don't know what will happen if you stay.'

'Oh, Conor. You're really nice.' She put her arms round him. 'Do you think I should go?'

'You know I can't see you in London?'

'You never do anyway,' she laughed, phone call, aunt Kate, Castletown Berehaven and London all suddenly very far away and unimportant.

It was not nice saying goodbye to Conor at Heathrow. They clung together and Alex felt a new desperation at facing aloneness again and Conor felt guilty about facing Karen. He hadn't even phoned her as he'd promised. And it was difficult not to want to go on seeing Alex. But they had agreed to keep the affair simple and uncomplicated – an interlude, which would become a self-contained memory of nice times shared. They held on to the happiness until the last possible minute, cuddling together under a blanket on the back seat of the jumbo, sharing a final joint seriatim in the toilet, and ordering a bottle of champagne just before landing.

But now they were standing outside the terminal building in the cold early morning. 'Wish I had a joint left for the taxi,' said Alex, brushing away a few tears. 'This is ridiculous. Goodbye and thank you very much for everything, it's been a pleasure working with you, or what the hell do I say?'

'Have a nice day you-all,' said Conor, Switzer-style, close to tears himself.

They'd decided to travel to London in separate taxis, and they were now holding up the queue. The waiting drivers started going on at them, so Alex grasped Conor's shoulders one last time and said 'bye' with a wry scowl of resignation on her face. She threw her two small bags across the floor of the taxi and got in after them without looking back. Conor stood and waved.

Alex missed him terribly at first, and lived in hope that he would phone. Jane was away apparently, and there was no one else that she felt like talking to. It was up to Conor to make a move, but maybe she should have pushed harder and not been so damn reasonable. But then again, much as she enjoyed his company, she didn't want to move in with him. She couldn't see herself taking Karen's place as co-owner of a run-down terraced house in Stoke Newington, and it was unfair to offer anything less.

But she quickly became more and more absorbed by the task of working up her notes on the trip into a form acceptable to the magazine, and by Wednesday she had just about regained her normal equilibrium. The affair with Conor was receding neatly into the sort of cameo-memory existence that they had planned for it. So as she walked over to her parents' flat on that mild sunny evening she was feeling relatively cheerful. There was a bank holiday towards the end of the month and she was thinking about taking a trip over to Castletown Berehaven for a short break. . . .

She stopped in her tracks. She was halfway up Queens Gate and the tall stuccoed buildings swayed above her, threatening to topple over and crush her. She wanted to run for safety but she was rooted to the spot. She stared up again and the tall houses were still there. It was the tall trees covered with new leaves that swayed, but the overwhelming panic remained, translated now into its true terms: Aunt Kate was dead, so she had no reason to go to Castletown Berehaven. There was no one special to visit anymore: Tom didn't count, he was just a friend like any other in so many other places. There was no special reason to visit Castletown Berehaven now that Kate was not there.

This is what death means, it suddenly struck her. Beyond the conventional sadness was this struggle with an egotistical unwillingness to adjust to the side-effects of loss that was seldom mentioned. One person gone, and everything shifts and those that are left are deprived. Castletown Berehaven had gone as well as Kate.

A simple cliché echoed round and round her head: 'Things will never be the same again, things will never be the same again.' The prospect was intolerable, yet she had to go on.

As she started to walk again she found herself repeating aloud, 'No, not Castletown Berehaven, I can't lose Castletown Berehaven.'

She pulled herself together enough to present herself at her parents' door with a sulky face, the expression of her new experience of mourning.

'Alex, dear. You needn't look so sad.' Her mother kissed her gently on the cheek and took her jacket. 'Of course it's awful to lose Kate so suddenly, but the more you think about it, the more you come to see it as a blessing in disguise. No lingering disease, no slow deterioration. She went very peacefully in her sleep.'

They joined Alex's father in the comfortable sitting room with its familiar sunlit view over Kensington Gardens, and her mother continued with a description of the wake, the removal, the requiem mass, as her father poured them each a glass of whiskey. Then she came to a sudden halt and looked at her husband.

'I'm really sorry I couldn't be there,' said Alex to fill up the silence. 'Did my flowers arrive?'

'Oh yes, they were lovely. But you could have asked me to get some for you on the phone. I suppose we just never thought of it. They came from a florist in Killarney for some reason.'

'Yes, I've never understood how it works, this Interflora stuff.'

Her mother gave another meaningful look at her husband, and he cleared his throat.

'We had a session with the lawyers on Monday. Liam's old firm. They're handling it all very well. She's made all sorts of arrangements.'

'Oh.'

'She's left most of her money to the Church. There was rather more of it than anyone expected.'

'Oh. That's nice for the Church.' A bit flippant, but what was she supposed to say?

'Apart from a few small legacies that is. Everything was very well organised.'

Alex noticed that her mother was smiling across the room and shaking her head in disbelief.

'What is it?' she asked them both.

'Go on, dear, tell her.' Her mother was laughing now, as her father cleared his throat again and said: 'She left the house to you.'

'WHAT?'

'You've inherited the house in Castletownbear.' Her mother was still laughing, and came across the room to give her a peck on the cheek. 'My dear, what a face! Cheer up, you're a woman of property now!'

Alex's mouth hung open, struck dumb for a few more seconds, then she threw her head back and laughed and laughed, while tears poured down her cheeks.

For once she accepted a lift home from her parents and the three of them drove the short distance in her father's Rover at a stately pace. Alex sat on the edge of her seat in the back, hugging her knees in a state of awful excitement. She invited them in for a nightcap to avoid being alone, but the flat was in darkness and her parents were afraid of waking Jane. She didn't tell them that she hadn't seen Jane since returning from the States, nor even heard from her. That sort of detail only worried them. They were in enough of a state already.

'Be sure to think things over very carefully, dear,' said her mother.

'And remember, Liam's old firm have said they'll act for you and give you any advice you want on the legal side. And you know that if there's anything we can do to help. . . .'

'Take your time about it, don't do anything rash, will you?'

She finally managed to get a word in between the two of them: 'I'm just going to play it by ear for a while. I can't quite believe it yet. I've no idea what to do, but I'll probably go over soon just to see what it feels like. Anyway, I wanted a break.'

A break from what? She waved at them solemnly as the car glided round the square and back towards Kensington. Then she did a silly little dance up the steps to the front door. A new key dominated her key ring: a heavy four-inch-long back door key, a duplicate of the one that Shanahan's were keeping for the lawyers. As Kate never used the front door it had no lock, but was bolted from the inside. Getting it open to remove the body had been an almighty operation according to her father. Tomás had helped. Alex was now very sorry to have missed the funeral. The Kerry Sullivans had sent women to keen and there'd been some great singing at the wake. It was only Kate's generation that got buried like that nowadays, she reflected sadly.

There was a note on the hall table – 'Darling, welcome back, see you later for a chat love Jane'. 'At least she's still alive,' Alex muttered, and went off to her room to fetch her journal, wondering what 'later' meant.

The drinks cupboard was exceptionally well stocked, which indicated that Jane must have some generous new admirer, perhaps a married man who preferred to meet her here. Alex decided to 'borrow' some whiskey and replace it the next day. This was no night for going to bed early and sober.

She very much wanted to phone someone up, phone every-one up, and spread the news. But when she narrowed it down to specific people to phone there was only Conor, who was out of bounds, and Andy who was still in the States. He'd moved on to L.A. and she couldn't remember the name of the hotel. She considered phoning Hugh, but stopped herself because there was the risk that his scepticism would force her into declaring a decision which she wasn't at all sure that she'd arrived at yet. And she felt too elated to phone Tom. It would be in bad taste since her mother had reported how helpful he'd been with the funeral arrangements, and how sad at Kate's death.

She'd known as soon as she'd heard about the house that she would go and live there – one day, sometime in the future when she was 'ready'. But that day could be a long way off. And then her father had distracted her with confusing details about what the house was worth on the open market (an enormous sum: the equivalent of a flat in Chelsea or a little terraced house in the inner suburbs) and then complications about taxes and not selling immediately and the deeds and her status as a non-resident Irish citizen. It seemed, and she said as much to her parents, that most of the apparent problems would disappear if she simply went over to Castletownbere and proceeded to live in the house. They were slightly horrified, but agreed that, in theory, that was one way to get rid of most of the legal complications.

Then her mother got worked up and started warning her against trying to make a living in the west, and talked about the advantages of London in terms of Alex's 'social life' and 'career' and brought out the old chestnut, 'What about your future?', which Alex always interpreted as, 'When the hell are you going to find a nice man to marry and settle down like everyone else?'

She smiled, remembering her parents' concern and how little she could say to ease it. If she tried to be truthful, as she had indeed done, it came out sounding like wishful thinking: 'I love it over there, I've often thought of going back to Cork, I've never expected to spend the rest of my life in London, I don't have a career, I just work, and I can work just as well over there – I can do things for the *Examiner* and RTE and all the Dublin papers – and don't forget I do have an M.A. – I can teach and I might want to do some research. Anyway I've got just as many friends around Cork as I have in London, besides all the cousins, I feel just as much at home there, and I love being near the sea, I never get bored if I can sail. . . .'

She felt silly, like a petulant teenage virgin trying to convince her parents that she'd come to no harm at an all-night party. In fact the whole scene felt like a re-run of her adolescence when she'd find herself arguing in favour of something only because her parents were against it, without any clear idea of what she really believed. And, as in that past phase, she didn't have any way of knowing whether her arguments would prove to be right. She shuddered as she remembered how happy she had been to get away from Ireland after her last trip, but then, she argued, that had been Kinsale, and London had been her working base. If everything was transferred to Castletown Berehaven then the confused emotions couldn't arise.

The one doubt remaining in her mind was whether the time was right yet, whether she'd taken everything that she wanted from London, or if she'd come to regret not having been more serious about her work and not having built up a more useful network of freelance contacts. Part of the trouble was that she'd never seriously considered basing herself in Castletown-bere if she moved to Ireland on her own. That possibility had only arisen with Tomás. Cork, or even Dublin at first, with long weekends in West Cork had seemed the only practical possibility if she were to go on working in what interested her. She saw that it was the half-hearted nature of that compromise which had stopped her from doing anything towards achieving it before now. If all she wanted from Castletownbere was long weekends, she'd be better off staying in London where she was doing well, and flying over whenever she could afford to, than uprooting herself to a new city.

The sensible course of action was starting to emerge. Before occupying her house in Castletownbere permanently she should spend another six months in London building up contacts, or even a year – who wants to move to the Beara in fucking December, she thought in panic. This was all becoming sickeningly serious. And how would she move her books? She'd have to buy a car. But could she spend another year, even another six months in London, knowing that at the end of it she was off to the Beara forever? Forever? Well, for as long as she could stand it . . . and wouldn't it be very likely that in the course of that year she would find some reason for prolonging London, or for settling there indefinitely? Wouldn't it be just typical of her luck that she'd fall in love with some fellow who had to live in London and they'd need the money from her house . . . GOOD GRIEF!

She pulled herself out of the fantasy in disgust, remembering, by vague association with the cussedness of luck, a conversation with Tom on the first night she'd met him. They were both up at the bar in Shanahan's talking with old Seany Harrington who was complaining about a run of bad luck saying that if he was still farming this would be the year that his ducks drowned. Alex only heard the last bit and asked Tom incredulously, 'Did Seany say his ducks drowned?' Tom told her that what Seany meant was that if it was raining soup at the moment, he'd have a fork in his hand. As Alex laughed at her own stupidity and the strange new expressions, Tom added: 'With Seany's luck, the day his boat comes in he'll be at the airport.' When Alex told him she'd heard that one before Tom teased her for being a townie, with another old saying, 'A joke goes a long way in the country.' That was when she'd first noticed how attractive Tom was.

Her mind was meandering. She would use the journal and work it all out in two columns – pro and contra. It was a method she often used when faced with difficult decisions. She opened the notebook and divided a page into two columns and wrote PRO at the top of one, and CONTRA at the top of the other. But she couldn't see what was supposed to be PRO or CONTRA so she crossed it out and started again on a new page with three columns: Reasons for going ASAP, Reasons for staying six months, Reasons for staying a year. Then she added '(i.e. indefinitely)' under the third heading, and looked at the page with distaste. It still wasn't right – it obviously didn't correspond to the chaos in her head, because she couldn't transfer that chaos on to the page.

'Ah.' Enlightenment was imminent. 'This is an "if and when" list. I need a "how" list because I'm definitely, quite definitely going, as soon as I sensibly can.' She added a mental parenthesis: 'And I'm not known for my sense as that blackguard Tomás would say.'

Excitement and elation again. It felt better in the rethinking. She wrote a new heading: *How to get AB to CTB (ASAP)*, then, inspired by a flash of the silly light-headedness that had been attacking her ever since she'd heard the news, she wrote: 'Buy a car, drive to Pembroke, and take the ferry to Cork.'

She was still staring at the page, awed by the simplicity of it, and doubting she'd ever have the guts to see it through, when she heard Jane's key in the latch. Jane was alone, and looked untidy and worried.

'Darling!'

'Jane! At last!' She stood up, and for the first time they embraced. They both started talking at once, Jane asking about the trip and Andy and Conor, Alex asking about Martin and David and Jane's art dealing. She offered Jane a whiskey, explaining about the borrowing and a private celebration, and acting mysteriously Jane-style. But Jane, who refused a drink with a grimace, was at it too. They recognised they were playing the same game and broke into laughter.

'I've got the most amazing news to tell you,' said Alex.

'No, I've got absolutely devastating news. You'll be stunned.'

'All right then, you go first.'

'No, you first. I want to know yours first in case it's the same sort of thing.' Jane stared at Alex, who had tied her hair into a funny knot on top of her head while she'd been thinking. 'You look dreadful, what *have* you been up to?'

'A rather emotional evening. Decisions and things.' Alex felt smug, and unusually self-important.

'Oh, my God, maybe it *is* the same.'

'I doubt it.'

'But it's good news? Work or home or lovers?' Jane knew about Alex's triple division of potential problem areas. Alex hadn't yet looked at her new situation in those terms.'

'All three, I think. A radical re-shuffle anyway.' Tomás as a neighbour – how on earth would they cope with that?

Alex was starting to get impatient at the impasse. Jane's news, she thought, would pale in comparison. She was in love again, or some rich and famous man (whom Alex would probably never have heard of) was chasing her, or she'd unknowingly bought a Monet which was about to be auctioned for millions. She decided to break the silence by giving a clue.

'My aunt in Castletown Berehaven died while I was in the States.'

'Oh, I am sorry. You were awfully fond of her, weren't you? She used to write to you all the time.'

'Yes. I should have taken a bit more notice of her really. I mean you always feel you didn't do enough when they were alive. You know.'

Shit. So trite. 'She died very suddenly in her sleep, so in a way it was a blessing.' This wasn't what she'd meant to say at all. 'Anyway, it's absolutely weird.' (Conor's word, dammit.) 'But I suppose with hindsight we should have known.' Her voice was getting gentle and wistful, it reminded her of Tomás. 'I've just got back from my parents and we're all a bit dazed because of what's happened . . . she's left me her house.'

Jane didn't react, so Alex tried rephrasing it. 'I've just inherited a house in Castletownbere.' That didn't have any effect either, so she put it in terms that she hoped would impress Jane: 'I'm rich. My aunt left me this superb house in the main square of Castletown Berehaven.'

'Is that your news?' said Jane, and in spite of the disbelief and wonder in Jane's face, Alex felt that her delayed reaction was belittling. Jane went on in the same tone: 'That's marvellous, really super for you. Are you worth absolutely pots now?'

'Pots and pots,' said Alex weakly, hoping the exasperated expression on her face would be taken for bewilderment, and rather doubting that her idea of 'pots and pots' was the same as Jane's. Luckily Jane considered detailed discussion of money to be sordid. And her mind was elsewhere:

'Well, that's all right then. Now you won't find my news *quite* so devastating.'

Jane leant back and scowled. 'Sorry. You'll understand in a minute.' She coped with what looked like an attack of indigestion, burping, or was it retching, behind her hand, then nodded at Alex. Alex was getting the idea.

'Yes,' said Jane. 'I'm pregnant. That's my news. Glorious, isn't it? I just feel sick as a dog most of the time.'

Alex said nothing. Jane's sarcasm made it difficult to answer. The two questions that occurred to her – 'who's is it?' and 'are you going to keep it?' – both seemed fraught with potential drama. So she said tentatively, 'Good Lord.'

Jane sighed and looked a bit happier. 'It comes in waves. The nausea. I think that's over now. Anyway, it's David's. Luckily I'm sure about that because I stopped taking the pill with Martin when it was all *on*, I was fending him off for weeks and then I had the curse just before we split up and by some amazing stroke of luck I haven't been with anyone except David since.' She smiled dreamily, and went on: 'I want the child, I really do want a baby, and' – a pause while she giggled – 'I think I've just agreed to marry David.' Another pause. 'But I'm not sure about that. I came home to think it over. What I expected was that he'd agree to support us and then I could give him limited visiting rights. To me I mean.' She laughed again. 'I feel like a real scheming bitch, but David's being absolutely super. He's just pointed out that he'll be sixty-three in August, and he's unlikely to last more than ten years, so if we do marry I'll only be about thirty-nine when he snuffs it, and after his other kids get their cut, I'll be rather well off. And the thing is he knows me so well, he knows all about my nasty habits and how useless I am and he still wants to marry me. He's convinced it's a boy, and he's never had a son, only four daughters. And three ex-wives. And he still wants to try again. Can you imagine?'

Alex couldn't. She liked David in moderation for his generosity and admired his razor-sharp intelligence in business, but he was also subject to fits of boring theorizing on marriage, women, sex and (worst of all) the evils of socialism. But it couldn't be denied that if he offered to marry Jane she would be foolish to refuse. He had a large flat in Belgravia, a country house in the Dordogne, and a business interest in a Caribbean hotel. Jane wanted children, she was twenty-nine and pregnant, and he was offering. Alex saw that Jane needed someone to celebrate the whole thing with her, to confirm the decision so that tomorrow Jane could get on the phone to broadcast the news.

'Jane, I think it's wonderful! David's a lovely man and he'll make you very happy. He'll make a wonderful father.' She was talking to the fireplace in front of her, and couldn't look at Jane who was sitting on her right. She knew she sounded like a text book agony aunt, but that was exactly what Jane needed. She went on: 'It probably isn't what you'd planned for yourself, but it'll be lovely in the end. I think it's wonderful – imagine a child of yours and David's – heeeee, congratulations, Jane, congratulations!' She got up and kissed Jane on both cheeks.

Jane sounded as if she was being strangled: 'Alex, do you know, you're the first person who's congratulated me?' She was crying now and clinging on to Alex's hands. 'I'm sorry, I get awfully emotional. But I've only told a few people and they've all said either "are you keeping it?" or "who's the father?". *Nobody*'s said congratulations. Nobody. Not even Pippa. Oh, Alex, I really will miss you when you've gone to Castletownwhatsit.'

'Well . . .' She couldn't bring herself to say, as she wanted to, that she hadn't yet really decided if and when (given a choice) she'd like to leave. All she knew was how, and she wasn't totally sure about that either.

Jane dried her tears and went on: 'David says I should let the flat, so he wants me to do it up properly, put in central heating and things, in fact they're coming round tomorrow to measure up' – Alex laughed openly at that – 'and then this woman he knows can let it for some phenomenal amount.' Then she mentioned Andy's landlady, which made the vague plans suddenly seem very real to Alex. Jane went on: 'I'm supposed to move in with David straight away so that they can get on with it, but I was awfully worried about you.' She sat up and looked as if she was preparing one of her bossy goodbye speeches. 'But now that you're off to Castletownwhatsit I don't have to worry at all. It's all fitted in so perfectly I can hardly believe it.'

'Neither can I,' said Alex faintly, with an irony that was totally lost on Jane.

She looked back at the journal which was sitting by her side on the Chesterfield, and showed Jane the clean new page with the heading *How to get AB to CTB (ASAP)* and the entry: 'Buy a car, drive to Pembroke and take the ferry to Cork', and said, 'This might take a week or two.'

'Darling,' said Jane, 'as long as you don't mind central heating chappies and interior decorators swarming all over the place, you can stay as long as you like. I mean, *at least* two weeks.'

RESOLUTION

'When the modes of music change, the state trembles.' So remarked Plato, and maybe he had a point. While changes in youth culture in Ireland have hardly brought down governmer they indicate how the country has become – almost unnoticed from over the water – something very different to either the rural arcadia or traditional tribal battlefield of British fantasy.

To start at the beginning. The Republic of Ireland now has the youngest population in the EEC. Until recently, the population of Ireland had been declining while that of other countries grew. Now, when many neighbouring countrie: show virtually no growth at all, the Irish population is rising faster than that of any other European country.

Population decline resulted from economic stagnation, for in the nineteenth century only the North-East corner of the island had been industrialized. Today it is the Republic that is booming – with an economy that has consistently shown the highest growth rate in the EEC. While all the urban areas have been expanding, increasingly people live in the big cities: with over a third of the population in the Greater Dublin area, the Republic is more dominated by its capital city than any other EEC country apart from Denmark.

Previously population had been adjusted to the meagre resources available by most people marrying very late, and many people not marrying at all (two gloomy indices on which Ireland used to head international league tables) – and above all, by mass emigration. By contrast, the 1979 census in the Republic showed a net immigration over the last eight years. Forms of sexuality and family life are also changing rapidly. More people are marrying and marrying younger; within the family they are increasingly using contraception to limit the number of their children. Consequently the earlier repressive climate of Irish family life is on the wane: something both signalled and accelerated by the sudden growth of the new music.

'Rock 'n' Roll in Ireland' – Extract from catalogue of multi-media exhibition, 'No Country for Old Men' (1980)

BEREHAVEN

Driving around the Berehaven Peninsula is a most pleasurable
and enjoyable experience and nowhere else is one likely to
encounter such breathtakingly beautiful scenery. Around
every corner and turn there is a new and delightful view
to delight and enchant the visitor.

CASTLETOWNBERE

Castletownbere is the capital of Berehaven and as such it
is a centre of much activity. This is a fisherman's paradise,
being Ireland's second largest fishing port and here many
specimen sea fish have been caught. There is fresh water
fishing also and there is much to see and do. Horseriding,
ponytrekking, windsurfing and sailing schools are some of
the sports possibilities. Nearby, Dunboy Castle is the
ancestral home of the O'Sullivan Beara and it stands in a
beautiful wooded environment. There is a ferry service
to nearby Bere Island where interesting sights include
nineteenth-century defences used to guard the British Fleet.

Ireland Holidays Southwest Cork –
Cork & Kerry Tourist Board, 1980

Alex sat in her pullman seat looking out across the grey-green sea at the colourless horizon, and down at the small foaming wave which bounced off the ship's side beneath her. Force two to three visibility moderate decreasing, she thought automatically, and smiled at the irrelevance of the information. The ferry's motors throbbed reassuringly under her and someone else was navigating.

It was a mid-week crossing in late June, and although the boat did not appear crowded Alex had been unable to get a berth. With a two-hour drive ahead of her in the morning and the task of unpacking the car single-handed and settling into the house, on top of the emotional wear and tear of the last fortnight, she could have used a good night's sleep. She had, understandably, been sleeping badly recently, waking up in the early hours of the morning either in a state of panic, or in euphoric elation.

She had come to believe that her mental health was directly related to her bank balance, which is why she always tried to keep a cushion of money on deposit in case of emergencies. After many hours spent doing sums in the journal and studying the pages of *Exchange and Mart* she decided that her need for a reliable car would have to constitute an emergency, and she spent all her savings on a second-hand Triumph Estate. It was hardly the car of her dreams, but it would get her, and most of her stuff, to Castletownbere, and if she needed ready money at any point she could take it over to Wales and trade it in for something older and smaller.

She was pleasantly surprised to find that, after buying the car and her one-way ticket, she had enough money, owed to her for work completed, to keep herself for about three months – four if she lived really quietly. 'Living really quietly' meant staying out of pubs, and she knew that was unlikely. She'd once been told that Castletownbere had one pub for every nine adults in its permanent population, and while that might have been an exaggeration, the town certainly boasted a huge variety of bars, out of all proportion to its size. That's about all it can boast, she thought, panic momentarily obliterating elation.

Given the discouraging reaction of the people around her it was surprising she had any elation left at all. Jane accepted her decision to leave London because it suited her, and because she'd always thought Alex was a bit nutty, and the move to Castletownbere was therefore typical. For that same reason, Andy also was unimpressed, and couldn't understand her excitement at what he saw as inevitable. Her colleagues had first assumed there was a man at the back of it all, and on being told that there wasn't, they then assumed that she had been building up to this for months, and must have a job lined up, or at least a circle of influential friends who would point her in the right direction. When they found that this was not the case either, and heard about her house, the general consensus was that she would be back in London by Christmas at the latest, repentant and chastened. People found her bland confidence that something would turn up rather irritating. The London correspondent of a Dublin daily had given her a couple of names to contact there, and the Sunday colour magazine had liked her piece on Andy and promised to commission a travel piece; beyond that she was on her own.

The worst reaction of all came from her mother, who now believed that Kate had deliberately left the house to Alex knowing that it would entice her away from a purposeful existence in London in favour of the kind of nothing life that Kate herself had lived in Castletownbere. Her mother couldn't even bring herself to name the place, but, like Andy, always referred to it as 'the back of beyond'. Such conjecture was unfair to the memory of a person as straightforward as Kate, a fact which Alex's father pointed out whenever he got a chance. But he too had his reservations about Alex's removal. Alex attributed their reaction to views which had become fixed for them some twenty-five years earlier when the impossibility of both being able to follow their respective medical specialisations, in a city as small as Cork was at that time, had sent them over to London. They'd done well out of London, and their lives, especially her mother's, would have been that much poorer both professionally and materially had they stayed in Cork. Cork was for them a place to retire to, and no one in their senses retired at Alex's age.

As Alex looked around the pullman lounge at her fellow travellers – all holiday-makers, some London Irish returning for their annual visit, some simple tourists – she had a new experience of superiority. She'd always felt special among people travelling to Cork, as if it mattered more to her, and she had some unique claim on the excitement of the experience. She hated the way that tourists appropriated Cork, seeing it as merely another place among many to be exploited for its potential holiday value, a new playground with quaint locals to be humoured, and splendid scenery, but a wretched climate which made the choice of destination a bit of a gamble. Now, for the first time, she was not travelling to Cork on holiday. She was going to Castletownbere to live.

Her state of mind was gradually becoming clearer to her, and as she watched the horizon she started to try to make sense of the contradictory moods that she had suffered from in the last two weeks.

It had been disconcerting for her to find that there was nobody, besides herself, who could understand what she was doing. Nobody could understand because she found it impossible to explain to anyone why she felt that moving immediately to Castletownbere was the right thing to do, and must therefore be done. There must be people, she believed, who would instinctively understand, but she didn't happen to know any in London. So she often felt that she was setting out on a wild adventure into uncharted territory with no rational justification, and that caused panic. Then she would remember that the place she was heading for was only a small fishing town in the west of Cork which she happened to know well and like. The fact that she also owned a house there was too much to absorb as yet. It was simply a pleasant but ordinary place where ordinary people lived quite unremarkable lives, reading newspapers, working, watching television and having a few jars in the evening. There was certainly nothing to be afraid of. She refused to consider the possibility that she might find small town life unbearably oppressive and boring. That point only arose when she lay awake semi-conscious in the small hours of the morning.

As for London, she had not renounced it forever. She couldn't imagine wanting to go back, but if for any reason she decided to do so there was nothing to stop her. She could find a flat, find work, renew acquaintances, admit that she'd been wrong to head west, and pick up the threads of her old life. So in a way she wasn't really taking a risk at all.

The elation and excitement came from her conviction that it was definitely going to work out, because she was doing the right thing at the right time. It probably wouldn't be what she expected – she didn't even know what she expected – but, whatever it was like, it would suit her. That was the adventure, that was the unknown, and it was already there waiting for her.

In her good moments the idea of settling in the 'back of beyond' achieved a romantic quality which she enjoyed as much as she enjoyed the chic simplicity (so admired by Jane) of her new address: Alex Buckley, Castletown Berehaven, Co. Cork.

She was off the boat before eight, and there was no point in waiting in Cork for the shops to open. She had decided she didn't want to encourage the habit of shopping outside Castletownbere, at least until she had some sort of income. Fresh coffee beans and French cheese and the variety of fresh vegetables available in cities were the only things she was expecting to miss, and she was determined not to let it matter. Instead there would be soda bread and locally killed meat, onions and cabbages from Seany's smallholding, new-laid eggs and unpasteurised milk still warm from Leary's cows left in a small pail outside her back door every morning.

It was a cloudy day, and there had been showers as the ferry came up the harbour, but now the sun was starting to break through. She drove slowly through a succession of small towns, their straggling main streets lined with multi-coloured cottages. The towns got smaller and sleepier as she travelled west, and the sparsely populated landscape became more and more beautiful: distant ranges of low, dark mountains, rough green land strewn with grey boulders, until finally she came to the sheltered bay of Glengarriff.

She didn't want to arrive too early, because in Castletown Berehaven, as in the rest of West Cork and Kerry, there were seldom people in the street much before eleven. She'd arrived at Glengarriff by ten, and Castletownbere was only half an hour down the road, so in a final gesture of celebration she stopped at the grand old Eccles Hotel for breakfast.

Hers was the only car in the car park, and she discovered in reception that they could serve her breakfast on the balcony which overlooked Bantry Bay. In her thick báneen sweater she was just warm enough. A couple of yachts rode at anchor, and when the sun came out from behind the clouds the sea sparkled and dazzled her.

It was a good breakfast: egg, sausage, tomato and a rasher the likes of which she hadn't seen for years. She chose soda bread instead of toast, and the coffee, served in a silver pot with hot milk in another, was so good that she lingered over a second pot. The sun was more consistent now and she was lapsing into a holiday mood, shedding the gloom and nervousness which had accumulated in her efforts to leave London.

She was served by a young girl in a pink T-shirt dress. An old dear in black with a white apron and cap would have fitted in better with the old-fashioned grandeur of the Eccles.

'Ye've grand weather for your holidays,' said the girl chattily as Alex settled the bill. 'I hope it keeps fine for you now.'

'Well, I'm not really on holiday' said Alex. She went on proudly: 'I live in Castletownbere.'

The girl fell silent, and looked at Alex mistrustfully. 'Castletownbere,' she said, obviously wanting to end the conversation, but not wanting to seem impolite. 'That's a very quiet place altogether.'

Alex caught her awkwardness, and couldn't think of how to continue the exchange. 'Yes. Well, goodbye now, and thanks a lot.' She could see, as she walked back to the car, that this was going to become, if not a problem, a minor irritation in her new life. She felt a bit of a fraud for not having given a fuller explanation, but it was difficult to explain without going into great detail. Yet she resented being labelled a tourist. She would have to develop some kind of jokey strategy for dealing with these situations. With her English car and her West Brit accent to guess she was on holiday was fair enough. And people around here liked holiday-makers, their trade meant the difference between survival and emigration to the city for many of the locals. And they genuinely enjoyed the bit of a chat.

Her new doubts quickly melted away as she concentrated on nursing the overladen Triumph along the rugged twisting road that led from Glengarriff down the side of the Beara peninsula. The same man from her local pub in Chelsea who'd helped her to choose the Triumph had also supervised the packing of it, and had insisted that she store most of her books and a lot of her records in his garage for the moment. She had only Irish poetry and novels with her, as it was the quickest way to choose a portable library without involving herself in a 'desert island books' ordeal. And it would be good background if she got any reviewing work from Irish papers.

Nevertheless, she had loaded the car down with her stereo, a selection of her records (mainly classical), a box of kitchen equipment, bed linen, some pictures and rugs and a mass of old journals and notes as well as all her clothes. On this, the last leg of her journey, she became absurdly superstitious and travelled at a maximum of twenty-five miles an hour, forcing herself to ignore the spectacular views of Bantry Bay which emerged at her left-hand side on every curve.

At last she rounded the final bend, then passed Brandy Hall, the first pub in Castletownbere. She drove slowly up the main street and into the square. Kate's house was on the first corner, and the back door was inside a small courtyard up an alley-way. She backed the car up the alley, and turned off the engine. Her hands stayed on the steering wheel, and she rested her head on them for a few seconds thanking St Christopher, whose medal dangled from her rear-view mirror, for her safe arrival.

She got out and stretched, then reached in through the open window and took her purse out of her handbag, which she left on the seat. The only people who locked their cars in Castletownbere were tourists. She crossed the road and wandered into the middle of the square, which was now used haphazard-ly as a car park. She stood beside the Celtic cross with her back to the new quay and the harbour, looking up at the row of imposing mid-Victorian houses facing her. Shanahan's, dou-ble the width of the others, had its door and shop fronts newly painted bright blue. She looked from Shanahan's down to the corner, Kate's house, the only one without a shop front in it. Seany Harrington had painted it a cheerful shade of turquoise two summers ago, and the elaborate plaster mouldings over the front door and downstairs windows were picked out in dark green. All the curtains were pulled, making it look blind.

Finally she allowed herself to look at Tom's house, between her own and Shanahan's. It had been newly painted off white, and a rough-hewn sign with black olde gaelic lettering above the shop window read 'Berehaven Inn'. Thank God it was a quiet, tasteful sign, she thought, all the while knowing that Tom would never have gone in for neon. In the shop window itself, which still had its old blind with the faded 'Sullivan' on it (very convenient) pulled half-down, there was a smaller wooden sign saying 'Pub Grub'. She kicked away a tattered plastic bag which a sudden gust of wind had driven against her feet, and crossed back over the road.

He'd installed a new front door too, a good solid half-door, not painted, but heavily varnished like the sign. She pushed it open and waited while her eyes adjusted to the gloom. There was a buxom rusty-haired woman with a ruddy face behind the bar, and one old feller in a corner with a pint.

'Hallo,' she mumbled as Alex closed the door.

'Hallo there. Is Tomás around?'

'He is. Who shall I say is asking for him?'

'Alex.'

She clattered up the stairs in her clogs and Alex heard a door open and shut and then open again almost immediately. She clattered down and scowled at Alex.

'He'll be with you in a minute now.'

'Thank you. And I'll have a glass of Murphy's please.'

Alex guessed from Tom's description that this must be the mountainy woman from the Dursey, and wondered, as a badly poured glass of stout was slammed down on the counter, if her surly manners were responsible for the emptiness of the bar, or whether she was getting 'special' treatment.

Tom had stripped out the painted wood cladding of the old interior and rebuilt the bar itself with a rough structure of weathered ship's timbers. The floor had red quarry tiles, and the grey stones of the wall were left exposed. There was a big fireplace and rope-seated chairs and bar stools were scattered around with barrels for tables. The only piece of furniture Alex recognised from old Hannah Sullivan's days was the settle which had been stripped down to its original oak.

It was almost a very nice bar: it lacked details like pictures and lamps, and gave Alex the impression of being half-finished.

There were footsteps on the stairs. She looked up and saw Tom standing behind the bar smiling at her. He burst out: 'Alex Buckley, plague of my life! You might have told me you were coming over.'

She smiled back. 'It was a bit of a sudden decision.'

'How long are you staying?' – Always that, or the same thing but worse: When are you going?

She shrugged and couldn't think of how to put it. Tom had picked up a whiskey bottle and didn't seem to expect an answer.

'What are you drinking? he asked.

'I've a glass of Murphy's here.'

'None of that rubbish now. We're celebrating. It's your first time.' He was pouring two glasses of Bushmills without a measure. Typical. If he knew what he was going to give her why did he bother to ask?'

'Well. What do you think?' he asked again. She was miles away. Think about what?

'Welcome to the Berehaven Inn. Sláinte.'

Oh, the pub. 'It's great, you've done a terrific job.'

'I haven't finished the lounge yet, it's back there, so we'll have more space for food, then we'll really get going.'

Tom had put on weight and his beard had got bushier. His eyes were bloodshot, and it struck her that he had just woken up. Nothing wrong in that, but neat Bushmills for breakfast? It didn't look good.

'You've brought the fine weather with you.' He peered out under the blind. 'It's a grand day for Allihies.' He twinkled at Alex. There was a hidden cove in the cliffs beyond Allihies where they used to make love.

She began protesting: 'Tom, I've got a car to unpack, I've got to air the house. . . .'

'Never mind that, we'll do it in no time between us. I was very sorry about your aunt Kate passing on, but as they say, it's an ill wind . . . and I want to welcome my new neighbour. Drink up now.' His tone changed to heavy sarcasm. 'Finola here will be happy to mind the shop for me for half an hour, won't she?' The whiskey bottle was snatched off the counter by Finola and placed on the back-shelf where it belonged with a thump. Tom started pushing Alex out of the door in front of him, telling her, 'She's the devil of a temper, you've got to watch these mountainy women from the Dursey. . . .' A wet dishcloth flew across the bar, catching Tom on the back of the head, followed by a highly imaginative oath, and as Tom threw the dishcloth back in the door he said to Alex with phoney gentility: 'Jeez, the problems I have with the staff.'

It took Alex a very long time to sort out the mess that resulted from that unloading of the car. Tom took charge, and everything was dumped in the front parlour, which she came to look on as a storeroom. Things stayed there until she felt a need for them, making her occupation of the house a gradual process.

At first Tom was delighted to find that she intended to stay indefinitely, but then he became concerned: 'You're crazy, do you know that? You'll never last the winter. Jesus, woman, where are you going to find work? How are you going to survive? Have you thought about that at all?' While Tom drove his open MGB towards Allihies at a fierce pace she shouted the best explanation she could manage: the truth, as usual with Tom.

He was silent, until he'd bought two whiskeys in Harringtons. Then, when they were sitting in the sunshine on the window sill outside looking out across the sea at the distant Skellig rocks, he made one of his very rare serious remarks.

'Alex Buckley, you're a crazy woman, but I hope to God it works out for you. You're doing the right thing, there's no question of that. But it won't be easy. Just remember, we're neighbours now, and whenever you need a helping hand you've only to ask.'

At last she'd found someone who almost understood. It was the nicest thing anyone had said to her since she'd decided to move. His gravity reactivated the panic, and quelled it at the same time, leaving her close to tears. She shook her head instead. 'Honestly, Tom, I'll manage, I'm used to looking after myself.' She had meant to be more gracious, and then she remembered that Tom had already bailed her out once in the past, and felt a bit foolish at mouthing clichés about self-sufficiency, so she added humbly, 'But it's grand to know you're there.'

It was an idyllic sort of day, her last idyllic day with Tom. As usual they had one drink in all four bars in the tiny village of Allihies, with Tom's old excuse that to leave any of them out might cause offence.

The cloud had lifted and it was perfect sunny weather with light breezes – a 'pet day', Tom called it. Tomorrow, he predicted, the rain would come down again. They took one of their drinks over to the stone wall beside the yellow water pump and leant against the horse's trough looking out across a green meadow to the cliffs and blue sea beyond. Tom talked about sailing over to the Skelligs sometime on the *Pico*. Landing was tricky except in certain wind and tide conditions. It was something they'd often discussed, but this time Alex knew she would be around long enough for them to carry it out.

At Eyeries, the next village, in Lynch's lounge bar, they met a young couple from Dublin who had moved down recently to work a smallholding just outside the village. Tom got involved in a detailed discussion of livestock and crops while Alex sat beside them, content to look out of the picture window at yet another view of green hills, low cliffs, grey rocks and sparkling blue sea. She was feeling very pleased with herself.

Simply to have arrived was a great achievement. To have no pressure on her to leave ever again made her dizzy with happiness. It was hard to believe that it was only yesterday that she'd left London. She raised her eyebrows acknowledging with difficulty that London was still booming away across the water, teeming with people who had not left for the Beara, and most probably never would.

She looked out again across the green meadow to the low cliffs and the deep blue sea. Here she had space, and she had time in hand to solve her material problems. She felt overwhelmingly privileged. And she decided then that for the next two months she would do absolutely nothing, and let time take its course and present her with the solution. It was a kind of act of faith in the resources of the new home that had been presented to her, and she felt it was the best way to express her gratitude.

A phrase drifted over from Tom's conversation, advice he

was offering the young couple about their land: 'Leave it fallow, leave it fallow as long as you can possibly afford to, then you'll reap the benefit.'

'My God,' she thought. 'Isn't it wonderful how the world fills with poetic patterns after a few drinks with Tom. That's exactly what I'm going to do for the whole of July and August: leave it fallow.' She would sleep, read, walk, sail, or merely sit and dream, she would have a few jars in the evenings, do anything she liked, except fret about The Future: leave it fallow.

She wanted to turn and tell Tom, but seeing the fresh-eyed way the kids were listening to his practical advice she recognised how irrelevant her decision about what to do with her freedom – i.e. nothing – would be to them. And she suspected she was a bit drunk.

By the time they reached their next port of call, the Holly Bar in Ardgroom, they were both definitely a bit drunk. Alex noticed that her watch said seven o'clock and wondered where the day had gone, and how Finola was coping with the 'half-hour' that Tom had said he'd be away for.

They took their drinks outside again and leant on another rough stone wall which spanned the road where a mountain stream from the lake above at Glenbeg ran under it. Rugged green countryside, grey rocks again, and on the banks of the brook grew clusters of tall purple foxgloves, the same beautiful flower that had lined the hedgerows on her way down from Cork. Was it only that same morning? She pointed them out to Tom and for the first time that day he took her hand.

'I suppose you won't change your mind now that you've seen the place?' he asked in his new soft voice.

She shook her head. 'I don't know what'll happen, but I hope we can stay friends.'

'We'll always be friends. And now we're neighbours too.' He squeezed her hand and let it go. 'I've a woman coming down from Cork next week to take over from Finola.' The new softness in his voice made him sound kind, but crushed.

'Oh.'

'I think you'll like her. She was teaching and she's sick of it, so if she can settle she'll stay.'

'Are you fond of her?'

'I could get that way. It's time I was married. I need a woman, and there's not many of them around here.'

So much fire and energy seemed to have gone out of him. He had an air of sadness, bereavement almost, permanently around him.

'Are you a bit down?' It was an inquiry she often made of her London friends, but with Tom it seemed intrusive, far too casual and banal for someone like him.

'I need a woman. I don't go in for talking about it much, but I suppose I get depressed. There doesn't seem to be much point to anything nowadays. It might be different if I had kids and someone to care for.'

This was very unlike Tom. Recklessly she decided to try and cheer him up, momentarily at least. 'Let's have one last night together, blast you,' she said, putting on her Kerry accent for the 'blast you', 'and then we'll just be good friends.'

'Plague of my life.' He cheered up enormously and hugged her. 'I don't know how you do it, no one else ever makes me talk about myself like that. Crazy woman.'

'Hey, you haven't said anything yet, you're going to say a lot more before I've finished with you. One last night. And then I'm going to become a celibate recluse and do absolutely nothing for two months.'

He laughed with all his former gusto: 'Jesus, woman, will you ever get sense?'

EPILOGUE

The Irish Celts possess on their own soil a power greater than any known family of mankind of assimilating those who venture among them to their own image. Light-hearted, humorous, imaginative, susceptible through the whole range of feeling, from the profoundest feeling to the most playful jest, passionate in everything, passionate in their patriotism, passionate in their religion, passionately courageous, passionately loyal and affectionate.

*The English in Ireland
in the Eighteenth Century*
J. A. Froude (1881)

Castletown Berehaven,
Co. Cork

Sept. 1

Dear Jane,

Many thanks for your letter – can't find it at the
moment as the sitting room where I write is in chaos. But I
was delighted to hear that the wedding went off so well
and your place in the Dordogne sounds wonderful! All
that sunshine and wine! I'll certainly try to join you there
next summer as you suggested, for at least three weeks –
that's assuming I can manage to get away!

Everything has turned out so wonderfully that I can
hardly believe it. I make no effort to sort myself out and
yet it just seems to get better and better. So much has
happened in the last few weeks that I don't quite know
where to start, and I'm afraid this will probably be an
immensely long letter. However, as you tell me David lets
you do nothing except lie in the sun all day, I hope it will
amuse you.

I may as well start with Tom as you asked about him.
We had a lovely day when I arrived, went straight off on
our ritual pub crawl round the Beara and ended up in bed
for one last time. He's got a new girlfriend – Joan – who's
doing the food for him. She's an ex-teacher and I get on
very well with her. Tom's very keen to marry her, but
she's a bit wary. Unfortunately Tom is on the bottle – he
gets depressed because he thinks it's time he got married
and had kids, so when he's depressed he drinks and the
more Joan sees him drink (he gets very cranky) the less she
feels like marrying him. . . .

Tom has been the most superb friend to me in all sorts
of ways and is a wonderful neighbour. It's much nicer like
that, and I know if I ever feel like moaning he'll be there to
listen, though he usually tells me off all the time (nothing's
changed really!). The amazing thing is that so far there's
been nothing much to moan about – one or two small

things, but nothing important. I'm deliberately cultivating a West Cork accent because I got so pissed off with people assuming I was on holiday, and it must be working because they ask me less and less nowadays. The other problem is to do with being a woman alone in a very small town. If I have any man in the house for more than ten minutes the whole town assumes we're having a lay – no kidding! – and now that I've actually had men to stay overnight my reputation is totally in shreds. Or so Tom tells me! It's very hard to take all this seriously, but there was a bit of a nasty incident last night which I will recount anon.

It all started about three weeks ago. I was very quiet up to then, just taking long walks and reading and playing with my kitten (a present from Tom that seems to have ended up with the name Old Soppyguts) and training for the sleeping Olympics. Then a Kinsale boat turned up with an old sailing pal of mine, Mick Roche, on board, and a couple of his friends. It was piss-awful weather for the next few days so all three of them stayed in the house in sleeping bags. We had great crack playing cards until all hours and telling stories. It just seemed logical at the time to ask them to stay, and I enjoyed the company. But Tom says it caused an awful lot of gossip, and I got some terrible looks when I went up to mass on Sunday. Luckily I never go to communion, or I might have got lynched! Anyway, Mick's great fun and I'm crewing for him in Schull next week.

Then there was Philip, an academic from Dublin who came down to do some research on an English historian called Froude. Funnily enough I'd just finished a book by Froude about a local character called Morty Óg (more about him later!) so when we met in Tom's bar Philip and I hit it off like a house on fire. He lectures at Trinity, and it seemed silly for him to be spending his research grant on B & B so I thought to hell with my reputatation (as old Seany calls it) and he moved in for a week. He went nuts about my uncle's collection of history books which is all I've been reading lately. His wife, an English sociologist called Annie, joined us for the weekend. She's very involved in the women's movement here, and has a great sense of fun.

It turns out she's a great friend of Madeleine Arnot who is in my year at school if you remember. I'm staying at their place when I go up to Dublin later this month. Philip thinks his publisher would be interested in a book on Morty Óg and his times, so I'm hammering out a synopsis. And Annie knows lots of good journalists and is going to introduce me around. She's sure I can pick up a lot of stuff like book reviewing and features that I can work on down here.

Before Philip arrived I had this perfectly amazing experience which totally knocked me out and not just because it was my first and only lover here and the best I've ever had anywhere! He's half-Spanish, half-French, a Basque in fact, and he's the skipper and owner of one of the trawlers that call in here. Tom was scandalized at first, even downright racist about it, but he now admits that José Maria (whom we've nicknamed Morty) is an 'ace feller' (his highest term of praise). I think it might be love, but for once I'm trying to hold back and be sensible. His English is very good, and he's even learning Irish (me too). He dropped out of university to join the merchant navy, and he has the most charming old-fashioned manners. But it's very hard to get to know someone in four days, especially someone so different from anyone I've ever met, and with this knee-crumbling physical effect on me. He's thirty-nine, but ageless-looking: quite stunning in fact, tall with longish dark hair and high cheekbones and the most beautifully proportioned body. He doesn't just walk, he sort of lopes everywhere, and is fantastically strong. The most weird thing is an obsession I've had with this local hero Morty Óg (who died in 1754) and I had a very strong mental picture of Morty, and José Maria could be his double! I nearly passed out the first time I saw him, it was the strangest way to meet, miles away from anywhere on a deserted cliff top, and mutual mistaken identity. It was even stranger seeing him in Tom's a few days later, like meeting a dream. He'll be back in town at the end of the month, and he's already invited me to the village near Coruña where he's living at the moment, though he says he's planning to settle in Ireland . . . sorry to rave on so much, but it's hard to get him out of my mind. It would appear I'm even being faithful to him, so it must be serious!

The one nasty thing (it was only last night) really did leave me a bit shaken up. It's this old guy I've known for years called Brady, who farms a smallholding just outside town. He insisted on seeing me home from the pub at closing time, and then he insisted on coming in. I thought he wanted a cup of tea, then when I turned round he pulled out his prick and said he knew I liked it – I suppose I was expected to tear off my jeans at the sight of such a glorious instrument. Yuch. In fact he tried to force me and kept saying, 'Will yer go?', but he was very drunk and I managed to push him out of the back door and then he fell over Old Soppyguts and I threw a pitcher of water from the rain barrel at him and he shot off up the street cursing like a madman! I went over to Tom's for a brandy, and he seemed to think I should have expected something like that the way I've been carrying on for the last few weeks, even though, apart from Morty, I've been living like a nun. Apparently Brady's only in his forties, and I'd always thought he was at least sixty-five. Tom thinks I should get a dog, but as I told him, with the performance Old Soppyguts put up, who needs a damn great dog! But it would be quite nice, either a labrador or a setter – much prettier, setters, but they tend to be a bit dim.

Apart from a v. super love life, which you are now entirely up to date on, I have a pretty good social life too. Philip and Annie introduced me to a great crowd of people on the other side of Bantry around Schull and Goleen and Ballydehob. There's a lot of writers and artists living there, and it's not a scene I ever had much time for (I used to think of them as ageing hippies) but I found they were great. And I have a lot of new friends in Castletownbere too. There's masses of young people around and there are discos and dances every weekend (I never go, but it's nice to know they're on!) and one of the bars has a huge video screen and they show really good movies and old Benny Hills – very tempting on a rainy afternoon!

Last week sixty-four trawlers ran in for shelter and the place was overrun with Spaniards and Bretons. They were great crack, and we all started wondering whether we were really in Ireland at all. Everyone reads a lot too, so we have plenty to talk about when we're not playing darts or singing! Maybe it's the people who've been the nicest surprise, but whatever it is, I'm certainly very happy and can see no reason at all for going back to London.

A feller in Tom's bar the other night told me a long long story about a man who married a woman whose father owned a pub, which ended with the moral: 'If your father's a poor man, nobody can blame you, but if your father-in-law's poor you must be plain stupid!' I thought David would like that – no offence meant!

Conor is coming over at the end of the month as the colour supp wants us to do a piece on traditional music on the west coast (Dingle and Clare, not L.A!). We'll probably keep it on a proper working basis this time, as since my experience with Morty I've totally gone off other men. If they're not as perfect as Morty there's no point. I tell you, this one is *really* serious!

Andy will be in Kinsale in December and I've promised to go up and stay with my parents at the same time so that he'll have a bit of company. I dropped in on him on my way back from Cork last week, having read about his presence here in the local rag. He's done a lot of work on the house, and it's looking very good. I'll probably go over to London after that to pick up the rest of my stuff and have a bit of a holiday. It's strange to be doing things back to front, going there for a break instead of coming here. But I must say I don't miss anything at all – I spent a hilarious evening in a bar in Ballydehob called Gabe's with some people who moved here from London two years ago making a list of 'Things We Don't Miss'. It had just about everything on it from the BBC to traffic lights! Apropos, I find I never use any make-up nowadays, except for keeping my toenails painted red to make me feel glamorous in bed!

Such trivia! There may be better ways to pass the time, but this seems to suit me perfectly. It's not at all what I expected, but I love it!

Look after yourself, you must be a magnificent size by

now . . . give a big kiss to David for me, and send me a further account of the wonders of pregnancy and married bliss ASAP.

pip pip
Love, A. B.

After a hard day's racing out of Roaring Water Bay Mick Roche and his crew decided to celebrate by dining out in Schull. It was a beautifully clear evening, but crisp with a touch of autumn. Alex wore white trousers and a white T-shirt ashore, but needed her dark blue guernsey as well. And, once ashore, she put on her high-heeled sandals, aware that it was probably the last time she'd use them this season.

The crew had a terrible thirst on them, and as they disappeared up the hill towards the nearest bar she shouted after them: 'A pint of lager!' She preferred to dawdle. She paused various times on her way up the hill to look back at the red setting sun and the yachts riding on their moorings in the harbour. She could still become momentarily dazed by the sheer beauty of her surroundings. And she was getting to like Schull more and more. It was far enough from both Castletownbere and Kinsale to guarantee her a relative anonymity.

Mick's crew alone could have filled Newman's without the locals and other racing crews who had already occupied the bar stools and the settle. The warm smoky atmosphere, the crush of bodies and the babble of voices was, as usual, almost overpowering after a day at sea.

Alex saw her pint sitting on the bar as she went in the door and stretched an arm between two old men to reach it. She took a long drink, watching the rest of the crew who were standing a couple of feet away from her in the crowded space between the bar stools and the settle. One of the old men she'd leant across for her lager tweaked her elbow. She turned around, and he whispered politely in her ear: 'I can see yer a lady. Willya sit down there?'

He pushed his bar stool towards her.

'No, no thanks, I'm with them over there. You sit down yourself now.'

'Oh no. I can see yer a lady.'

He pulled her towards him by the elbow. He was a short, bandy-legged man, peaked cap, dark shiny jacket, a weather-beaten face with far-sighted blue eyes and a crooked mouth which was either smiling or leering at her. Alex decided that he was probably a good twenty years younger than she had assumed at first, and the Brady incident flashed across her mind.

'Not again,' she thought.

'Come on here now.' He beckoned her closer to him. She could hear one of the crew accusing Mick of bad tactics as they'd tacked around the Fastnet and she was itching to join the discussion.

'What?' she said impatiently, about to move away. The smile/leer was growing, and he whispered in her ear: 'Yer either a lady or a whore.'

'WHAT?' Indignant at first, then guilt and shame from an irrational suspicion that this stranger had second sight and, like the Ancient Mariner, was compelled to reveal the truth to chosen victims.

'I sez if yer not a lady yer a whore. It shows.' He looked down and she followed his glance. The leer turned into a good-natured smile: 'Any woman paints her toenails, she's either a lady or a whore. That's a fact.'

Alex looked up at the ceiling and laughed in delight at his old, old joke. The petty worries of the last few weeks and longer-established doubts, the detritus of years of misjudged decisions and impulsive experiments, disappeared. She sat on the bar stool and drew herself up straight with a new grace and confidence. She knew she was all right. She had arrived.

'Sláinte,' said the man, pleased with the effect of his joke.

'Sláinte,' said Alex, and added with a gratitude so strong that it ruined her accent: 'Agus go raibh maith agat.'

'Ta fáilte romhat, aléanabh.'